African Adventure

Hal felt the full crash of the leopard's body against his own, striking him with such force that he tumbled backwards into the water . . .
Instinctively he gulped a lungful of air as he and the beast plunged beneath the surface. He felt the savage claws tearing at his clothing and biting into the flesh.

Hal and Roger, on safari in Africa, are annoyed when their attempts to capture wild animals are made even more difficult by a bogus 'White Hunter' they have to take along with them. But they soon find that their greatest danger is from an evil Witch Doctor, leader of a secret brotherhood of killers, the Leopard Society, which is determined to kill the Hunt brothers . . .

African Adventure

Willard Price

Illustrated by Pat Marriott

KNIGHT BOOKS
Hodder and Stoughton

First published in Great Britain in 1963 by Jonathan Cape Ltd.

This edition first published 1971 by Knight Books

Nineteenth impression 1990

Printed and bound in Great Britain for Hodder and Stoughton Paperbacks, a division of Hodder and Stoughton Ltd., Mill Road, Dunton Green, Sevenoaks, Kent TN13 2YA (Editorial Office: 47 Bedford Square, London WC1B 3DP) by Clays Ltd, St Ives plc

ISBN 0-340-14904-3

Contents

1 | Leopard in the night

HAL woke with a start. He found himself sitting up in bed, his spine tingling. What had roused him? A cry of some sort.

The play of light and shadow in the tent told him that the camp-fire outside was still burning. It was meant to keep off dangerous visitors. Wild animals were all about – yet the sound he had heard did not seem the voice of an animal.

Still, he could be mistaken. This was his first night in the African wilds. Beside the camp-fire earlier in the evening he and his younger brother, Roger, had listened to the voices of the forest while their Father, John Hunt, told them what they were hearing.

'It's like an orchestra,' Hunt had said. 'Those high violins you hear are being played by the jackals. That crazy trombone – the hyena is playing it. The hippo is on the bass tuba. Doesn't that wart-hog's "arnk-arnk-arnk" sound just like a snare drum? And listen – far away ... you can just hear it, a lion on the 'cello.'

'Who's that with the saxophone?' asked Roger.

'The elephant. He's good on the trumpet too.'

A sharp grinding roar made the boys jump. Whatever made it was very close to the camp. It sounded like a rough file being dragged over the edge of a tin roof.

Roger tried to cover his fright with a joke.

'Must be Louis Armstrong,' he said, and the others laughed rather uneasily. It did sound like the gravel voice of the famous jazz singer.

'Leopard,' said Hunt. 'He sounds hungry. I hope he doesn't come any closer.'

But the sound that had made Hal sit up stiff and startled in his bed was none of these. Now he heard it again – a piercing shriek, followed by the screams of men and women and the barking of dogs. The noise seemed to come from the African village on the hill just behind the camp.

He heard his father's cot creak. Roger remained fast asleep. Thirteen-year-olds do not wake easily.

'Better see what the trouble is,' said John Hunt. He and Hal pulled on their clothes and went out. The African scouts and gun-bearers who had been sleeping around the fire were awake and chattering excitedly.

There was a rushing through the grass just outside the zone of firelight. Hunt put his ·375 Magnum to his shoulder. He lowered the gun when he saw that what was emerging was no wild beast but the headman of the village with three of his men.

'Bwana,[1] quick, help us,' he called as he came running, 'The leopard. It has taken one of the children.'

'Come on, Hal,' said Hunt. 'Joro, Mali, Toto – get your guns and come along.' And to the headman, 'Did you pick up its trail?'

'Yes. It went down towards the river.'

'Get a couple of flashlights,' said the senior Hunt. Hal plunged into the tent to grab the electric torches. A sleepy voice came from Roger's bed.

[1] Bwana=master.

'What's up?'

'We're going hunting.'

'What?' complained Roger. 'In the middle of the night?'

Hal did not wait to explain. He dived out and joined the men already on their way up the hill. Knowing his adventurous younger brother, he was not surprised when Roger came panting up behind. He was still in his pyjamas, having taken time only to put on a pair of boots.

At the edge of the group of thatch-and-mud huts angry villagers milled about, men shouting, women wailing, children crying.

Here the headman pointed out the leopard's trail. Hunt played his torch on the tracks and led the way down the hill towards the river.

Hal noticed that a woman was accompanying them.

'Why is she coming?'

'It was her child,' the headman said.

Half-way down they came upon the child's body. The leopard, frightened perhaps by the commotion, had dropped it and fled. The bare brown skin was deeply cut by teeth and claws, and oozed blood. The woman, with a little cry, gathered up her child. Hunt felt for the pulse.

'Still alive,' he said. And while the sobbing mother turned back to the village with the unconscious child in her arms, Hunt again took up the trail.

'No time to lose,' he said. 'It could have gone a mile by this time. Or it might be lying just here behind a bush, waiting for us. That's one thing you can always expect of a leopard – it will do the unexpected. Watch out.'

He stopped, puzzled, where the footprints were indistinct. John Hunt, explorer, collector of wild animals for zoos and circuses, had had long experience in tracking animals – yet he didn't claim to know everything. The best tracker in Africa is not the white man but the African, who from childhood has learned to interpret every turned pebble and every bent blade of grass. The official tracker in Hunt's safari was big black Joro, and Hunt now called his name.

'Joro, take a look at this.'

There was no answer. Hal swung his light on the men. There were the headman and the three others from the village, there was Mali, and there Toto. And the camp dog, a big Alsatian named Zulu. But no Joro

'I thought I told him to come,' said Hunt.

'You did.'

'He acts strangely sometimes. Well, no matter – I think this is the way,' and Hunt led on down the hill.

Hunt's flashlight, strapped to his forehead to leave both hands free in case he had to use his gun, threw a strong shaft of light on the pug marks. Yet John Hunt hesitated. Something was wrong with these footprints. Certainly they had been made by the feet of a leopard. There was no mistaking the imprint of the four oval toes and the large triangular heel. But at the tip of each toe-print was a deeper dent, evidently made by the claw. That was odd, because a leopard has movable claws which come out when he is attacking but are drawn back into the toe when he travels. This looked more like the trail of a cheetah, whose claws are always out.

'But it can't have been a cheetah,' he said to Hal. 'A cheetah would never enter a house and grab a child. These are a leopard's tracks all right. But the claws wouldn't be out – not unless the beast was dead.'

'Dead,' Hal repeated. He wondered. Could the tracks have been made by dead feet? The idea was fantastic. But this was a land where the fantastic was commonplace.

His sharp eyes noticed something else.

'Dad,' he said, 'there are no blood-stains along this part of the trail.'

His father stopped and gazed at Hal thoughtfully. That was curious. After clawing the body, the leopard's feet had left a little of the child's blood in every print. But now, suddenly, there was no more blood. The feet would get dry, but not so quickly. There should be a trace of blood left. He knelt and examined a print at close range. There was not the slightest speck of red. He grinned up at Hal.

'You'll be a tracker yet.'

But Roger wasn't going to let his nineteen-year-old brother walk off with all the honours.

'There's something else,' he said. 'When we were after that jaguar down on the Amazon – remember? – it slid along close to the ground – pressed the grass down flat. Doesn't a leopard do the same?'

'Yes, it does,' admitted his father.

But here nothing of the sort had happened. The grass stood up two feet high between footprints.

Hunt shook his head.

'Beats me,' he confessed. 'But we can't solve the mystery by standing here. Let's get along.'

They went on down the slope at a half-run. The headman came up beside John Hunt and poured out the troubles of his village. This was the third child the leopard had taken in the last ten days. The first two had been killed. Every time the leopard grew bolder. The people of the village lived in constant terror.

'You will kill it?' he pleaded.

'I didn't come to Africa to kill animals,' John Hunt

said. 'I want to take them alive. But a man-eater deserves
to be shot. Don't worry – we'll get it one way or another.'

They entered a grove of trees and bushes along the river
bank. On they went with tense nerves, knowing very well
that the beast might spring out at any moment from a
patch of grass or brush, or might drop from an overhang-
ing limb.

'What's that – over there, near the doum-palm?' said
Hal. His father directed his forehead light towards the
spot. Something was moving, something yellow with dark
blotches. Now it stood out plainly, and it was certainly
the hide of a leopard. But the thing seemed to be erect like
a man. It was leaping for cover. Just before it disappeared
from sight it looked back at its pursuers. Its face was a
man's face, but so poorly lit that one could not clearly see
the features.

Now it was gone. The hunters reached the place where it had been seen, and fanned out in all directions. But the beast, or man, or whatever it might be, seemed to have vanished into thin air.

2 | The leopard-man

EVEN the tracks had disappeared, hidden by the tangle of brush and grass. No one knew what to do next. The men from the village plainly did not want to go farther. A leopard was bad enough. But a leopard that could change into a man was an evil spirit. It could appear and disappear at will, and no gun or arrow could hurt it. So they believed, and trembling with fear they were ready to call it a night and go back to the village.

'But how about your children?' Hunt said. 'Are you willing to let them be taken, one after another?'

'There is nothing we can do,' said the headman. 'And nothing you can do. A leopard can be killed, but not a leopard-man. Come – you will return with us to the village. You have lights – we dare not go back in the dark. Listen, he laughs at us.'

From the depths of the wood came a harsh, grating, coughing sound that only a terrified imagination could interpret as a laugh. It was like the rasp of a saw through coarse wood.

'That fellow, whoever he is,' said Hunt, 'can certainly give a good imitation of a leopard. I'm going after him. You can come along, or stay here, just as you like.'

He and the boys set off in the direction of the sound, and the Africans unwillingly followed. Scrambling through brush, over logs and around trees, they chased the 'evil spirit' and hoped it would not be there when they arrived. The two torches, worn by Hal and his father, cast their beams far in among the trees, searching for something in yellow and black.

Hal stopped. 'I think I see him. Up on a branch, just to the left of that ant-hill.'

Hunt strained his eyes. Yes, he could just make out something yellow and black, probably the skin disguising the figure of the leopard-man.

The dog Zulu growled softly and began to run ahead.

'Wait, Zulu,' Hunt ordered. 'Come back.' The dog reluctantly obeyed, still growling.

'Now that's strange,' said Hunt. 'When we saw the leopard-man before, Zulu was quiet. Now she's all excited. Why the change?'

'If we go straight for the leopard-man he'll run, just as he did before,' Hal said. He took off his light and gave it to Roger. 'Stay here and keep the light shining on him. I'll sneak round and come up behind him. I think I can wrestle him off that branch. And I have a knife I can use if necessary.'

'Don't use it unless you have to,' said his father. 'Remember, this is just a man and we have no warrant to kill him. I must say his actions are suspicious. But all we can do is arrest him and turn him over to the police for questioning.'

The headman objected. 'Your son must not do this. He is strong, but he has no magic. The leopard-man will turn into a leopard and kill him.'

But Hal had already crept out into the dark and was making a wide circle round the crouching figure on the branch. Hunt had little fear for his safety. He knew that his six-foot son, with muscles like steel springs, stood a good

chance against any human enemy. As for the notion that
the leopard-man might turn into a leopard, he had no
patience with any such superstition. He noticed that
Zulu had followed Hal. The two of them should be able to
give a good account of themselves against the mysterious
stranger.

The impatient dog kept pressing on. Hal warned her.

'Easy, Zulu, don't be in a hurry.'

Now they came out on the river bank. The stars glinted
down on the smooth surface. Those slow-moving masses
on the other shore were hippos. Almost under Hal's feet a
crocodile that had been resting with its head on the bank
switched about and dived.

They came up silently behind the tree. It was an ancient
baobab with a huge trunk, probably hollow inside. They
slipped round it until they could see the dark form on the
branch. A strong smell penetrated their nostrils. Hal remembered the same smell in a zoo coming from the
leopard's cage. But, he reminded himself, this was no
leopard but only a man.

The eager dog went into action first. With a savage
growl she leaped for the branch. At the same instant the
thing on the branch leaped at the dog and they met in mid
air. Hal realized with a sickening shock that this was no
human being but a full-grown leopard. Zulu would not
last ten seconds under those terrible jaws and claws. The
two animals fell to the ground, the leopard's teeth around
Zulu's neck.

Hal drew his knife and closed in to rescue the dog. The
two bodies whirled about so fast that it was hard to dis-
tinguish between the dog and the big cat. Hal's knife
might find the wrong animal.

Then a strange thing happened. The leopard, with a

howl of pain, released its jaws from the dog's throat. Zulu's collar, covered with heavy, brass studs as sharp as nails, had saved her. The points had stabbed the palate of the leopard and made it relax its hold.

Now it turned on an enemy it could hope to conquer more easily, and Hal felt the full crash of the leopard's body against his own, striking him with such force that he tumbled backwards into the water. The impact had sent the knife flying from his hand. By instinct he gulped a lungful of air, just as he and the beast plunged beneath the surface. He felt the savage claws tearing at his clothing and biting into the flesh. He knew that a leopard's claws can do far more damage than a lion's, because a lion mauls with his front feet only, while a leopard uses all four at once. And teeth as well.

Probably his father and the others were now on the bank, but there was little they could do to help. He must work this out for himself. He hooked his foot under a waterlogged branch that lay on the river bottom, and so

held himself and his quarry under water. Could he drown
the beast? Or would he himself drown first?

He had had a good deal of experience during his under-
water adventures in the Pacific. From his Polynesian
friends in the South Seas he had learned how to last a good
three minutes without coming up for air.

He had no idea whether a leopard could do better than
that, or not so well. He clutched the animal's throat,
trying to hold the head well away so that the powerful
jaws could not reach his face. But he could do nothing
about those ripping claws. Curiously enough, they did not
hurt. Later on they would – and plenty.

Staying down three minutes without exertion is one
thing. Staying down three minutes while locked in a life-
and-death struggle with a big cat is something else. Hal
was getting winded. But the leopard was not doing too
well either – the fight had almost gone out of it and now it
was only anxious to get away. Hal grimly held on. His
enemy's struggles grew weaker. If he could just hold the
creature down one minute more . . .

He had forgotten about the crocodiles. The swish of a
powerful tail close by reminded him. A crocodile would
ordinarily think twice about attacking a man – but
attracted by blood it might think only once, or not at
all.

Hal loosed his foot and came to the surface. His head
emerged and he took air, but he still held the leopard's
head under water. A beam of light from the shore struck
him and he heard his father's voice. Then both his father
and Roger leaped in beside him and hauled him ashore,
his hands still gripping the motionless leopard's throat.
They dragged the beast up on to the bank and Hal put his
hand over the heart. The leopard was dead.

'How about you?' Hunt asked. 'Did you get badly mauled?'

'Only scratched,' Hal said, still too excited to feel his wounds.

The Africans were happy and terrified. Happy that the killer of their children was dead, terrified that it might come alive again in human form.

The limp body lay on the river bank. Not one of the Africans would touch it. When Roger went towards it the headman said sharply:

'Keep away. It is still full of magic.'

Hunt studied the worried face of the headman.

'You really believe that, don't you? You went to a Christian mission school, you speak English, you learned something about science – and you are afraid of a dead leopard.'

'My friend,' smiled the headman, 'not all wisdom is to be found in school. Our knowledge is passed down to us from our father and grandfathers. We have always known what you have learned for the first time tonight – you have seen it for yourself. The leopard became a man and the man became a leopard. And all the time it was neither man nor leopard, but an evil spirit.'

Roger, under the spell of the night and the strange things that had happened, was staring at his father with open mouth.

'Perhaps there's something in it, Dad. It's all been so crazy I could believe almost anything.'

His father grinned. 'I don't blame you. But perhaps it isn't quite as mysterious as it seems. I think I'm beginning to see through it. You remember when we were following the tracks from the village and they became lost in the grass, and when we found them again they seemed pecu-

liar. At the point of each toe-print there was a claw mark.
But a live leopard doesn't keep his claws out when he
walks. Those prints were made by dead feet.'

Roger's jaw hung a little farther open. Was his father
going a bit barmy?

'Dead feet,' his father went on. 'The paws of a dead
leopard strapped to the feet of a man. You remember that
the grass wasn't flattened down as it would be by a
leopard. It stood two feet high, as it would if a man's legs
had brushed through it. That man was trying to mislead
us so that we shouldn't find the real leopard. Later we saw
the man – dressed in a leopard skin.'

'But why – why should he try to lead us off – and why
does he dress like a leopard?'

'Because he belongs to the Leopard Society. That's a
band of killers. It's not so active here in Uganda, but we
are very close to the Congo border and it's strong in the
Congo and all through Central and West Africa. It's a
very secret society. When a man joins it he is given a
leopard skin to wear, leopard's paws for his feet, and steel
hooks strapped to his fingers so that he can claw his
victims. He is taught that he can actually change into a
leopard at will. And since he belongs to the leopards, he
must defend all leopards. He must kill anybody he is
ordered to kill. Especially he must kill anyone who kills a
leopard.'

Roger's forehead was puckered with the effort to understand all this.

'So he led us off the leopard's trail,' he said. 'Then we
saw him – and he ran. But when we found him again he
had changed into a leopard.'

His father smiled. 'He didn't change into anything. He
was a man, and is a man. Then we heard the real leopard,

and Hal stalked it. And there it is.' He glanced at the dead animal on the bank.

'And where's the leopard-man?'

'Who knows? Probably skulking around in these woods waiting for his chance to do us in for killing his brother beast.'

'A comforting thought,' said Hal. 'Let's get out of here.'

3 | Mystery of the missing tracker

A s they turned to go, a flash of one of the lights revealed
two more leopards – but very small ones – emerging from
a hole in the trunk of the baobab and running to their
dead mother to suckle. Mewing like oversize kittens, they
nuzzled against the quiet, wet body.

'Poor little duffers,' Hunt said. 'We'll take them back to
camp and see if we can't fix up some substitute for
mother's milk.'

'Let me carry them,' said Roger. 'Will they claw
me?'

'Not likely. They're too young to be afraid of you.'

Roger, a little gingerly, with a proper respect for both
claws and jaws, gathered up the two babies, one in each
arm.

'And we'll take the big cat too,' Hunt said. 'Some
museum will be glad to get that skin.' He signalled to the
Africans to take up the body. When they showed no sign
of obeying, he did not press them.

'Well, Hal, it's up to us.' He drew some cord from the
pocket of his bush-jacket and tied the feet together, while
Hal found a fallen branch that could be used as a pole.
The pole was run through between the looped feet, and
with Hal at one end and his father at the other, the 100-
pound cat was raised from the ground and began its
journey to camp. The two lights were kept sweeping here

and there, on guard lest the leopard-man should be lying in ambush.

'And how about the male?' said Hal. 'Isn't he apt to pounce on us when he sees us carrying off his family?'

'A male lion would be after us in a minute,' said Hunt. 'But a male leopard isn't a family man. After he's started things off, he lets mamma take care of the children and herself. He's probably miles away, hunting.'

Roger, carrying the cubs, was suddenly startled by a cold nose against his wrist. He expected to feel teeth next, for this must be the father of the cubs. Should he drop the little animals and run? He peered down into the gloom. The animal he saw was not quite like a leopard - no, it was just the big Alsatian, Zulu.

The dog was a handsome female, owned by Mali. Though a lady, Zulu was every bit as strong, courageous and beautiful as a male. And she went beyond a male in her affection for anything small on four wobbly legs. Before coming on this safari, she had had to leave a litter of pups. Unable to mother them, she now seemed to want to mother the leopard cubs, and kept sniffing at them and nuzzling her nose into their fur as she trotted alongside.

It was a relief to come out of the dangerous dark into the warm glow of the camp-fire lighting up the circle of tents.

'Bring a cage for the cubs,' Hunt said. 'A large one, so they'll have plenty of room to play.'

Mali and Toto hauled down a lion cage from one of the trucks. Hunt padded a large clothes-basket with a warm blanket and pushed it into one corner of the cage. Then the cubs were introduced to their new home. Just before the door was closed, Zulu slipped into the cage.

'Come out of there,' commanded Mali. But the dog whined and retreated to the far side.

'Suppose you let her stay,' suggested Hunt. 'Let's see what she has on her mind.'

Mali closed the door. Zulu, with ears cocked forward, studied the two balls of fur. She sat on her haunches and seemed to be lost in thought. Then she came forward and sniffed at each in turn. They did not seem exactly like pups, but they were just as helpless. Certainly they needed somebody to look after them.

She went over by the basket. Looking back at the cubs, she gave out a series of little yipping barks which plainly said, 'Come here!' The cubs did not understand. They lay quiet and frightened on the cold, hard floor of the cage.

With a business-like air, Zulu walked to one of the cubs, gripped the fur at the back of the neck in her teeth, and lifted the squirming animal from the floor. She seemed to find it a bit heavier than she had expected. She carried it to the basket and laid it down on the blanket. Then she brought the other cub and laid it beside the first. There was still room in the large basket for herself. She stepped into it, lay down in a half-circle, and drew both cubs against her. After a protesting mew or two, they snuggled close to her, evidently enjoying the warmth of her body, because an African night, even near the Equator, can be cold.

In the meantime Hunt was treating the scratches on Hal's arms and chest. Luckily Hal's heavy bush-jacket had prevented the claws from going very deep.

'Just scratches,' Hal said. 'Never mind them.'

' "Just a scratch" from a leopard's claw can be serious if it isn't attended to,' his father told him. 'The claws can be highly poisonous, because the leopard eats dead animals and particles of the decaying flesh remain in the claws. Hold steady.'

He cleaned out the wounds with boiled water and applied a strong antiseptic. Mali returned from a search in the bushes with some leaves and roots which he proceeded to pound until they gave out a thick, white milk. This was smeared on as a poultice and covered with bandages.

But one cut in the left arm was too deep and wide for such treatment. It had to be sewn up, and Hunt, searching through his medical kit, discovered that his supply of catgut thread needed for sutures was exhausted.

'We will use ants,' suggested Mali. Hunt had often heard of this art, for it is practised by primitive tribes all over the world, but he had never seen it done. He watched with great interest as Mali poked into one of the ant-hills so common in Africa and stirred up the white ants, better known as termites, until the warriors rushed out. He seized one of these and squeezed it until its jaws opened

wide. With skilful fingers he drew together the edges of the
cut in Hal's arm, then placed the open jaws one on either
side of the cut, where they bit savagely like two pincers,
completely closing the wound. He broke off the ant's
body, leaving the head in place and the jaws locked. They
would remain locked until the wound healed, when the
ant-jaw stitches could be removed.

More ants were used in the same way until a row of
heads extended the full length of the cut. Hal and his
father looked on with admiration as the skilful black
fingers put the last ant-clamp in place, then applied the
milky poultice and a final bandage.

Wounds so treated generally heal without difficulty, but
Hunt took the added precaution of giving Hal a strong
hypodermic injection of penicillin.

No one thought it worth while to go to bed, for dawn
was already streaking the east with rose and silver.

One of the mysteries of the night had not yet been
solved. What about the tracker, Joro? He had been
ordered to go along on the hunt. But when he was needed
to read the tracks, he was not there. Why had he stayed in
camp? Or *had* he stayed in camp?

'Tell Joro I want to see him,' John Hunt told the cook,
who was going round from tent to tent with cups of steaming coffee.

'Joro is not here, *bwana*.'

'But he must be here. He didn't go with us.'

The cook seemed surprised. 'He wasn't with you?
Where else could he have been?'

'That's exactly what I want to know. There he is now.'

The cook turned and looked across the camp ground.
Joro was just coming out of the bushes. Evidently hoping
he would not be seen in the half-dark of dawn, he crept

like a cat to his tent and slipped inside. As usual, his chest
and back were bare, his only garment a well-worn pair of
safari pants. He seemed to carry some sort of bundle
under his arm.

Ask him to come here,' said Hunt.

When Joro came, Hunt was impressed by the drawn,
haggard face and hate-filled eyes of his tracker. It was not
the first time he had noticed this bitterness in the man's
face, but it had never been so marked as now. But Joro
was a good tracker, and this was the first time he had
definitely disobeyed orders.

'Joro,' said Hunt, 'I asked you to go with us last night.
Didn't you hear me?'

Joro answered sullenly, 'I didn't hear you.'

'Where were you all night?'

'Here, of course.'

'But they say you were not in the camp.'

'They are mistaken. I was in my tent, asleep.'

'But I saw you come out of the brush just a few minutes
ago.'

'Yes, *bwana*. I went out early to look for you.'

Hunt saw that this line of questioning was getting no-
where.

'Joro,' he said, 'what do you know about the Leopard
Society?'

That question went home. Joro was visibly shaken. His
voice was unsteady as he replied, 'I know nothing of it,
bwana.'

It was plain that he was deeply disturbed. Hunt was
sorry for him. He could not answer this man's hate with
hate, for he was not a hating man. He realized that Joro
was somehow in the grip of terrible forces and the good
and bad in him were struggling against each other. Here

was a man to be pitied and helped, not feared or fought.
Joro, shifting uneasily from one foot to the other, said,
'May I go now?'

'Joro,' said Hunt kindly, 'you are in trouble. You don't
want to tell me what it is. That's quite all right. But remember, in this camp you are among friends. If you ever
need us, all you have to do is ask.'

'I won't need you,' Joro said with a sudden flash of
anger, and left the tent.

4 | Cubs' breakfast

HUNT went out into the morning sunshine and breathed deeply. The air was sweet with the scent of dew on the grass and all the better for the fragrance of bacon and eggs cooking over the open fire. Hal and Roger joined him. Together they looked at the miracle that is fresh every morning in the African big-game country.

In the low rays of the just-risen sun the animals were coming down to the river to drink.

Animals, animals, animals, of every shape and form, animals by the hundred, by the thousand, were on the move.

'I never dreamed it would be like this,' Hal said.

'No one can believe it until he actually sees it,' said Hunt. 'Every time I come to Africa it strikes me as hard as it did at first. You often read nowadays that wild life is disappearing, and it's true in a way – but you can see that there's a lot of it left.'

'Looks as if all the zoos in the world had just been let loose,' said Roger, as he made a complete turn-about, his eyes sweeping over a sea of bobbing heads, every head containing the same thought – breakfast.

Nibbling at shrubs or high grass as they went, or seizing smaller animals if they were meat-eaters, they ambled down towards the river. On the other side of the river, too, they could be seen coming down from the hills to meet at the river's bank.

Hunt pointed out those that passed close to the camp, and named them. The big eland was cram-full of dignity and majesty. The graceful, streamlined impala was full of fun, jumping six feet high over bushes instead of troubling to go round them. The ungainly wildebeest (in crossword puzzles it is called the gnu) flounced about awkwardly like a fat old lady trying to do the twist. The little duiker (which means diver, because he dives through brush) did not go round bushes like the stately eland, nor leap over them like the impala, but plunged straight through.

And still they came – zebras frisking like horses, long-faced hartebeest, springing klipspringers, dik-diks almost small enough to put in your pocket, waterbuck, bush-buck, kob, oryx, and those lovely gazelles which they would see all over East Africa, the Grants and the Tommies.

A giraffe went by, his long neck angling into the sky like a derrick. He paused to pick some tender young leaves from the top of a tree. Then he went on to the river. How would he get that high head of his down to the water?

The giraffe lowered his head, but even when it was as far down as he could get it, it was still several feet above the surface. He knew by instinct how to solve that problem. He spread his front feet wide apart so that his body slanted down from tail to neck like the roof of a house. Then his lowered head easily reached the water. Every gulp ran up his neck in a bulge as big as a cricket ball.

'Lions!' exclaimed Roger. Two big, tawny beasts with heavy manes, who looked as if they belonged in Trafalgar Square, walked along with heads down.

What seemed strange to Roger was that gazelles and waterbuck a few feet away from the lions paid no attention to them.

'Why aren't they afraid?' asked Roger. 'I thought all animals were afraid of lions.'

'See those sagging bellies?' Hunt said. 'The lions have eaten during the night. They are full and satisfied, and the antelopes know it. So why should they be afraid?'

One of the lions let out a sudden roar that seemed to shake the ground. Roger expected to see him spring upon one of the passing animals. Surely his father must be wrong; a roar like that must mean business. But the animals still gave no heed to the King of Beasts. Hunt saw the bewildered look on his son's face.

'A lion roars *after* he has had his dinner,' Hunt said. 'Perhaps it's his way of saying thank you. It means he is satisfied, content with himself and with the world. If you hear a lion roar during the night, you don't need to be scared. It's the lion that doesn't roar that you need to be afraid of. When a lion is hungry he creeps up on his victim without making a sound.'

Until now all the animals had politely gone round the camp, not through it. But suddenly two huge black objects that seemed as big as locomotives came blundering straight into the camp ground. They squashed one of the tents, and two Africans popped out of it squealing with terror. The two monsters went straight on through the camp-fire, kicking pots and pans in all directions and spattering eggs, bacon, and coffee over themselves and the astonished cook. Out they went on the other side and down through the bushes to the river. A troop of terrified baboons fled out of their path and went galumphing into the woods where the leopard and her cubs had been found the night before.

It is easy to scare an African, but after the danger is over he just as easily laughs. And now the whole camp rang with laughter over the confusion that had been caused by the two living locomotives.

As they cackled and giggled, they went to work putting up the badly battered tent, and the cook collected his

kitchenware, raked together the scattered embers of his fire, and started all over again to prepare breakfast. But everyone kept a sharp eye out for more rhinos.

'Why did they barge through the camp?' Hal wondered.

'They probably didn't even realize there was a camp,' Hunt said. 'Rhinos are just about the stupidest animals in Africa. They have very poor eyesight. Those two brutes probably didn't see the tents or the fire. They simply knew there was a river down below, and nothing was going to stop them from getting to it.'

A plaintive mew came from the cage of the baby leopards. The dog had been let out earlier to take her morning run. Now she was back, looking into the cage and whining softly. The two cubs stood on their hind feet,

with forefeet clawing the wire screen as they looked out at
her and mewed.

'How about breakfast for the cubs?' said Roger.

'That's a bit of a problem,' his father said. 'They need
their mother's milk, but since she is dead we'll have to
mix up some powdered milk. Then we'll warm it a little
over the fire.'

This was easily done. But it was not so easy to work out
how to get the warm milk into the cubs. Some was poured
into a dish and placed inside the cage. The cubs smelt it
eagerly but evidently had no idea of how to lap it up.

'What we need is a couple of feeding-bottles with rubber nipples that they can suck, just as they have been used
to feeding from their mother. But I'm afraid we won't find
anything like that in camp.'

'Can't we spoon-feed them?' said Roger.

'We'll try it.'

Roger opened the cage and drew out one of the cubs. It
wriggled and snarled, but did not try to bite or extend its
claws. Roger held it firmly while his father placed his
hand beneath the jaw, and pressed his thumb into one
cheek and fingers into the other. That would open a cat's
jaws, or a dog's. But the leopard's jaws were too strong
and remained tightly closed.

Now Hal got into the act. While Roger held the animal
and his father poised the spoon, Hal took hold of the
upper and lower jaws, confident that he could pull them
apart.

They would not budge. All the strength of the small
animal seemed to be concentrated in those jaws.

Suddenly it wrenched its head about and sent the milk
flying. Milk dripped from the little whiskers, but the jaws
were still clamped shut.

Hal laughed. 'Funny thing, when three big men can't make one small cat take its breakfast.'

Zulu was nuzzling the ball of golden brown fur with her nose and whimpering softly.

'What's the matter, Zu?' said Roger. 'What are you trying to say?'

Hunt studied the dog. 'I think I know,' he said. He called Mali, the dog's owner. 'Mali, didn't you say that Zu has just had pups?'

'It is so, *bwana*.'

'Then perhaps she's still in milk. She seems to have adopted these little rascals. Perhaps she wants to feed them. Put the cub back into the cage, Roger, and let's see what happens. Leave the door open.'

Zu, with a little bark, followed the cub into the cage, put one and then the other into the basket, got in herself, and lay down.

But nothing happened. The small animals turned away from the dog. One of them began to climb out of the basket.

'They need a little coaching,' Hunt said.

He went into the cage on his knees, took both cats by the nape of the neck, turned them about, and pressed their noses close to the food supply that was waiting for them. The cubs tried to wriggle out of his grip. When they found they could not, they relaxed. Their sense of smell gradually won them over to this unfamiliar foster-mother and they began to lick, then to suckle greedily.

Hunt could now let go and crawl out of the cage, and the cubs' breakfast continued with many little gurgling sounds of satisfaction. Roger was about to close the cage door, but his father said, 'I don't think you need to. Now

that they know where they can find their dinner, they
won't run away.'

When their meal was finished, the two cubs stretched
themselves out contentedly and purred like organs. The
dog began to lick their woolly hides.

'Getting their morning bath,' Roger said.

'It looks like that,' Hunt replied. 'Actually what it
does is to massage the muscles and aid digestion. Many
animal mothers do it by instinct, without knowing why –
dogs, leopards, lions, antelopes, and others.'

Roger admired his two pets – he considered them his.
Their fur was like dark gold. They didn't look much like
leopards. The circles and spots that mark the grown-up
leopard were as yet only soft blurs – they would appear
more plainly as the animals grew older. The whiskers, still
short, would become long and bristly. The greenish-yellow
eyes were fierce, but not so fierce as they would be. The
teeth and jaws were already bigger than a grown man's.
But the way each little cat staggered around on awkward
paws showed that it was still very much of a baby.

'Can we keep them until they grow up?' Roger asked.

'No. They will have to go to a zoo where they can be
cared for properly. Grown leopards don't make good
pets.'

'Why not? These little fellows aren't bad-tempered.
They haven't put their claws out once. And a leopard
doesn't grow very large – like a lion.'

'But they don't keep that sweet disposition when they
get older,' Hunt said. 'No matter how kindly they are
treated, they finally turn savage. A lion or an elephant can
be your friend for life – but not a leopard. Something in
their nature makes them suspect and hate everything else
that moves. And the leopard is very strong. Zoologists say

that it is the strongest animal for its size on earth. A leopard is a wonderful climber. It can run up a tree as fast as you can run on the level. When it kills an animal, it drags the body up a tree and puts it in the cleft of a high branch so that lions and hyenas can't get at it. Many times game wardens have reported seeing a leopard shinny up a tree dragging a waterbuck or a zebra three times as heavy as itself. Sounds impossible, but they've proved it by shooting the leopard and weighing the carcasses. And a leopard is more bold than other animals. Ask the villagers. They are more afraid of the leopard than of anything else. A lion won't come into a house, and an elephant can't - but a leopard thinks nothing of creeping in through a door or window and seizing the first living thing it finds.'

'Then why don't the game scouts go out and kill all the leopards?'

'A good question,' his father agreed. 'The answer is that in the scheme of nature the leopard has its place. For one thing, it keeps down the baboons. The leopard is very fond of baboon meat. If it weren't for leopards, there would soon be such vast numbers of baboons that every farmer's field would be stripped clean of every growing thing, and troops of baboons would become so bold that they would make raids upon village people and kill hundreds of them. That very thing has happened in parts of the country where there were no leopards.'

Roger swatted a tsetse fly that had lit on his hand. He looked at his father with mischief in his eyes.

'Well Dad, if everything is good for something, tell me what's good about a tsetse?'

Hunt grinned. 'You think you've got me there, you young rascal. All right, I'll tell you what's good about a tsetse. First I'll admit it's the most dangerous fly in the world, because its bite can give you sleeping sickness. That can happen, but usually doesn't – most tsetse bites are harmless. But the good thing about this bad fly is that without it you wouldn't be looking now at thousands of wild animals. They just wouldn't be here.'

'How's that?'

'I remember once I was making a trip through the Tsavo game reserve with the warden and I swatted a tsetse. He said to me, "Don't kill the tsetse. It's our best friend. Without the tsetse we wouldn't have any game park." I understood what he meant. The Africans raise millions of cattle and the cattle roam all over the land eating the grass right down to the roots, so that there is nothing left for the wild animals. But there is one place where the cattle can't go. They can't go into any area inhabited by tsetse flies, because the tsetse bite is deadly to cattle. So those parts of the country are left for the wild animals to enjoy.'

'But don't the flies kill the wild animals, too?'

'No. The wild animals have been living with the tsetse for so many hundreds of years that they have become immune to tsetse bite – they are used to it, and it doesn't hurt them. You notice this village has no cattle. That's because this is a tsetse belt. Of course cattle are good to have, but it's also good to have some places left where the most wonderful animals in all the world have a chance to exist.'

Roger looked at the dead leopard which the men were beginning to skin. 'Too bad we had to kill that one.'

'Yes. But when they become man-eaters, we have to do something about it.'

'Who gets that skin?'

'The American Museum in New York has ordered one.
If they don't want it, some furrier will be glad to get it.'

'What's it worth?'

'About two hundred and thirty pounds.'

'How many skins like that does it take to make a fur
coat?'

'About eight.'

Roger whistled. 'That makes a coat cost eighteen hundred pounds.'

'More than that. The furrier wants to make a profit. He
would sell a leopard-skin coat for two thousand five hundred pounds more or less, depending on the quality of the
fur. This fur was out of fashion for a while but now it has
come back strong. Probably because it's hard to get.
Leopards are becoming scarce. Of course, nobody needs
to pay that much to keep warm. A lady with less expensive tastes can buy an ocelot coat for thirteen hundred
pounds, cheetah for one thousand pounds, jaguar for three
hundred and fifty pounds. Leopard fur is the strongest
and most durable.'

Breakfast was ready now, and the hungry hunters fell to
with a will. Zulu came out of the cage to get her share.
Everyone was much too interested in bacon and eggs and
hot biscuits and coffee to notice the cubs until Roger
cried:

'They're out. They're running away.'

But the little leopards were not running away. Instead,
they waddled in pursuit of their foster-mother. They rubbed against her legs and licked her fur. They sniffed at her
dish of meat and turned away. This was not their idea of
good food. They were friendly little beasts. One of them
scrambled up into Roger's lap and licked his face with a
tongue that felt like coarse sandpaper. In no time at all it

had rubbed off the skin and drawn blood.

'Ouch!' cried Roger. 'You're just too good to me,' and he pushed the woolly ball down into his lap.

But the little bundle of energy showed surprising strength. He threw off Roger's hand and leaped up on the camp table, one paw splashing into Hal's fried eggs and the other into a cup of coffee.

He was captured and placed on the ground, where he set to work licking off his wet paws.

In the meantime, the other cub had disappeared.

'It can't be far away,' Hunt said. 'Look in the tents.'

The men dived into the tents and searched in corners and under cots and even in the canvas bath-tubs, but found no cub. They came out and searched the grass and bushes around the camp, with no result.

Then Roger happened to look up into the foliage of a tree that stood just inside the circle of tents. There was the cub, lying perfectly still on a low branch, watching with bright eyes as these silly humans ran here and there hunting for him. Now he really looked like a leopard rather than just a ball of woolly fur. His little claws gripped the branch. There was an almost savage blaze in his yellow-green eyes. He was ready to spring on anything passing below. This was something he had never been taught, but something that leopards had done for thousands of years, and the instinct was planted deep in his nerves and brain.

5 | The unlucky Colonel Bigg

IT was just Colonel Bigg's bad luck that he should choose this moment to walk into camp. The leopard, perched high where he could get a good view, was the first to see him. The mischievous little beast crouched low, dug his claws into the branch and prepared to leap upon the newcomer.

Colonel Bigg did not see the ball of fur on the branch. He saw only the tents and a fire and men. And he smelt bacon and eggs. And he was hungry.

While he was still hidden by the bushes, he stopped to spruce himself up. He removed his hat, took a comb from his pocket, and combed his hair. He smoothed the kinks out of his hat, replaced it on his head, and tipped it at just the right angle. After all, he was a White Hunter, or pretended to be, and must look the part. He straightened his bush-jacket and brushed the dust from his safari shorts.

He puffed out his chest like a pouter pigeon and tried to look important. That was not too easy, since he was not important. It so happened that Colonel Benjamin Bigg, White Hunter, was not a colonel and not a White Hunter.

He had owned a farm in Northern Rhodesia, but he was not a good farmer. He had gone bankrupt and lost his farm. While he was wondering what to do next, a man suggested, 'Why don't you become a White Hunter?'

It was an exciting idea. He, a White Hunter!

When a wealthy American, or German, or anybody, wants to go hunting big game in Africa, he hires a White Hunter to go with him, a man who knows the country, knows where to find the animals, and knows how to shoot.

When out on safari (a hunting trip) it is the White Hunter who bosses the expedition, sees that the camp is supplied with food, tracks the elephant or buffalo or lion, and tells the sportsman when to fire. If the sportsman only wounds the beast and it charges him, it is the White Hunter who must save his client's life by bringing down the enraged beast with a bullet in the heart or brain. When the sportsman poses for his picture with rifle in hand and one foot on the dead beast, the White Hunter has the right to pose beside him.

It's a proud life, a wonderful life. Who wouldn't want to be a White Hunter?

'But it's not for me,' Bigg said. 'I don't know a thing about hunting.'

'Now don't tell me that,' said his friend. 'Haven't you ever shot anything?'

'Only a jack-rabbit. And it got away.'

'No matter. You don't need to be able to shoot. Your client will do the shooting.'

'Suppose he misses?'

'Tell your gun-bearers beforehand to be ready to shoot. Then if your sportsman misses, you and your gun-bearers blaze away all at the same time. One of them is bound to hit home, and who's going to say it wasn't you?'

'But I wouldn't know where to take anybody to find game.'

'What of it? Your Africans will know. Leave it to them. Let them do the work and you take the credit.'

It sounded good. Bigg smiled. 'How do I get started in this racket?'

'Put an advertisement in one of the sport magazines. You know – "Professional hunter, long experience, expert shot, results guaranteed" – then give your name and address. Oh, there's one more thing. You ought to have a handle to your name.'

'Like what?'

'Captain or major or something. Makes it easier to sell yourself. Gives you class.'

Benny Bigg thought it over. If captain would be good and major better, then colonel would be still better. So he became Colonel Benjamin Bigg, White Hunter.

His advertisement in *Outdoor Life* brought a radiogram from a wealthy New Yorker: 'State price for thirty-day safari.' He must have been wealthy, since he did not back down when Bigg replied with a quotation of seven thousand dollars for his expert services for one month.

Bigg's offer was accepted. Bigg instructed his client to meet him in Nairobi, where most safaris are outfitted.

The client, Hiram Bullwinkle, together with his wife, arrived at the time set. In the lounge of the Norfolk Hotel they met the famous hunter to whose skill and daring they were going to trust their lives for the coming month.

Colonel Bigg played his part to the limit. He casually referred to his exploits during the war (he didn't say which war) and tossed off the names of some of his former clients, such as the Archduke of Austria and the King of Norway. Mrs Bullwinkle was entranced with this romantic hero of war and wilderness. Mr Bullwinkle was impressed, but a little uneasy. Somehow this professional hunter seemed a little *too* good.

Bigg went to an outfitting firm which did the things he

didn't know how to do for himself. They got for him the necessary game licences, experienced African gun-bearers and trackers, food supplies for thirty days, tents, cots, and folding bath-tubs, jeeps and Land-Rover.

So the safari took off, the clients guided by the 'colonel', the 'colonel' guided by his Africans.

For the first week everything went fairly well. Mr Bullwinkle bagged an elephant. His own bullet merely wounded the beast, but the gallant White Hunter and three black gun-bearers all fired at once and the elephant dropped dead.

It was odd that a monkey in a tree fell dead at the same moment. Colonel Bigg explained that one of his gun-bearers was not a very good shot. But Mr Bullwinkle remembered that the White Hunter's gun had most curiously wobbled about and at the moment of firing seemed to be pointed rather above the elephant's back and directly towards that monkey.

A waterbuck, a wildebeest, and a zebra were added to the bag, but each time there seemed some doubt about the White Hunter's part in the act. Mr Bullwinkle, who had some knowledge of men, began to suspect that his White Hunter was a fraud.

Then came the day of the lion. Mrs Bullwinkle ventured a hundred feet from camp to get a shot at a Tommy gazelle. She carried a ·275 Rigby, which was just right for a gazelle but not for big game. She was not afraid, for her White Hunter was beside her and he carried a ·470 Nitro Express, which was tough enough to tackle anything alive.

· What should pop out of the elephant grass but a huge male lion! He gazed for a moment at the two advancing hunters; then, since he was not looking for trouble, he turned to go. Mrs Bullwinkle knew her gun was not built to shoot lion.

'Get him!' she whispered. Colonel Bigg glanced around. His gun-bearers were not close enough to help him this time. Anyhow, there was nothing to fear. The lion must be a coward. He was running away. What a feather it would be in the colonel's cap if he could bag this lion! Bigg raised his heavy gun and fired.

What happened then scared him out of his wits. The lion, wounded just enough to become angry, wheeled about with a savage growl and came straight for his tormentor.

Colonel Bigg dropped his gun and ran for his life. Mrs Bullwinkle stood her ground and fired. With a final leap the big cat was upon her, teeth and claws tearing into her flesh. She heard another explosion, then knew nothing more.

She woke to find herself on her cot in the tent. The senior gun-bearer had just finished treating and bandaging her wounds.

'What happened?' she said.

'This man got in a shot just in time,' said her husband. 'The lion is dead.'

'Where is Colonel Bigg?'

'Gone. I sent him packing. I told him if I ever see him again I'll kill him.'

'But we can't get back to Nairobi without him.'

'Nonsense. Our Africans will get us back. They've been the brains of this trip all along. Do you realize you'd be dead now if it hadn't been for this gun-bearer? Bigg ran like a scared rabbit and left you to the lion. White Hunter indeed! He's a fake and we're lucky to be rid of him.'

So Colonel Bigg wandered for three days and nights

before the smell of eggs and bacon led him to the Hunt camp.

He did not arrive unobserved. Roger saw him stop to comb his hair, set his hat at a rakish angle, and take on the air of a big White Hunter. Roger also saw the crouching cat on the branch. And the stranger saw Roger.

'My boy,' he called. 'I want to see your master.'

Roger didn't like to be called 'my boy' and he didn't care for that word 'master'. With mischief brewing in that innocent-looking head of his, he came forward and stopped just short of the half-hidden leopard. To reach him the stranger would have to pass under the branch.

'Good morning, sir,' Roger said politely. 'What name shall I give my – master?'

The stranger drew himself up to his full height. 'Colonel Benjamin Bigg, professional hunter.'

'Who is it, Roger?' came the voice of John Hunt.

'A very important person, Dad. You'd better come.'

Hunt joined his son, and would have gone on directly beneath the branch to shake hands with the visitor if Roger had not stopped him with a hand on his arm. The newcomer repeated his name and rank.

Hunt thought he knew all the White Hunters, but he had never heard of this one. But he only said:

'You are welcome. What brings you out so early in the morning? Is your camp near by?'

'It is not, sir. I was guiding an American fool and his wife, who is a bigger fool. I rescued them repeatedly when their own folly led them into danger. They would not obey my instructions. Therefore I cancelled my contract and sent them back to Nairobi.'

'And you?' Hunt said. 'You struck out alone? No car, no gun-boys, no supplies?'

'Think nothing of it,' replied Bigg loftily. 'I know this country like the palm of my hand. And so long as I have this' – he tapped his rifle – 'I won't go hungry. Plenty of game about, and I'm not a bad shot.'

'Then I suppose you've already had your breakfast?'

Bigg looked beyond Hunt to the fire and the breakfast table, and his mouth watered.

'Well, well, I'll sit with you if you like, but I won't promise to eat anything. I'm pretty full.' He patted his stomach. 'Nothing like a buffalo steak grilled over an open fire.'

'So you killed a buffalo this morning? Pretty tough customer for one man to tackle.'

Bigg swelled up like a bullfrog. 'After you've been in this business as long as I have, you forget how to be afraid.' He took a step towards breakfast. 'No, no, I don't scare easily.' He took another step. He was almost under the branch. Roger prayed silently. 'One more, just one more.'

Bigg took one more step. Then he let out an unearthly scream as a snarling something came down on his head, making him stumble and fall. He dropped his gun, wildly waving his arms and legs to rid himself of this horrible beast, all the time shrieking and yelling as if his last moment had come.

Hunt picked up the baby leopard and helped the terrified man to his feet. When Bigg saw the size of the wild beast that had attacked him, he turned red. Hunt pretended not to notice.

'You will at least have a cup of coffee,' he suggested, and led the way to the table.

Bigg had little to say as he put away six eggs, eight rashers of bacon, ten helpings of hot breads with butter

and honey, and five cups of coffee. Hunt, realizing that his
guest was really hungry, had the cook broil a large antelope steak. Bigg made short work of it. Then, after a few
more cups of coffee, his self-importance showed signs of
coming back.

'By the way,' he said, looking about, 'Who is your
White Hunter?'

'We have none,' Hunt said.

'What? No White Hunter? You *are* in a bad way.
Where do you come from?'

'New York.'

Ah, thought Bigg, another innocent New Yorker. Bigg
had fooled one New Yorker – at least for a week – perhaps he could do better with this one.

'A city man,' said Bigg. 'The streets of New York are
hardly the place to learn about big game, are they now?'

'I suppose not.'

'So you know nothing about hunting?'

Hunt smiled. 'A little.' He did not think it necessary to
explain that he was not just a city man. He had a house in
the city but spent most of his time at his animal farm in
the country. There the wild animals gathered in Africa,
India, and South America were held until they were
bought by zoos, circuses, or carnivals. And he did not
think it necessary to say that after many safaris in Africa
he knew more about big game than most White Hunters.
He could not only shoot animals, he could take them
alive, which is much more difficult.

And his sons were also good hunters. In the Amazon
jungle, under his direction, they had taken alive many
strange creatures, including the giant ant-eater, the tapir,
the anaconda (largest of all the world's snakes), and the
jaguar. In Pacific waters they had captured the great sea-

bat, the giant squid, and the octopus, and had gone deep
into the sea in search of pearls and the treasure of sunken
ships.

'I'll tell you what I'll do,' said Bigg grandly. 'You need
me, that's plain, and I won't fail you. It's lucky that I just
happen to be free. I'll guide you, and it will cost you very
little – let us say only three hundred pounds a week. But
mind you, I can't do it for long, I have too many other
important engagements coming up.'

'No thank you,' Hunt said. 'I wouldn't think of taking
up your valuable time. I hope you have a safe trip back to
Nairobi.'

Panic seized Bigg. He dare not go out again into that
wilderness full of ferocious animals. If they did not get
him and give him a quick death, he would die slowly of
starvation and the vultures would pick his bones. As for
Nairobi, he had not the faintest notion whether it was
north, south, east, or west. Somehow he must manage to
stay under the protection of this safari.

Hunt saw the anxiety in his visitor's eyes. His heart
melted. Hunt was naturally kind to animals, and no less
kind to the human animal. He had no liking for this big
bluffer, but he could hardly turn him out at the mercy of
the risks of jungle and plain.

'We don't need a White Hunter,' he said. 'But if you'd
like to remain with us as a guest until we get out of the
game country, we'd be happy to have you.'

Bigg felt as if a great load had been taken from his
shoulders, but he was careful to conceal his relief.

He pursed his lips and nodded slowly, as if giving the
matter great thought. 'I'm a pretty busy man,' he said.
'Still, I can't desert you, after seeing the trouble you are
in.' He waved his hand airily. 'Forget the fee. I'll stay with

you a few days at least if by doing so I can render you a service.'

The best service you can give us, thought Hunt, is to keep out of our way. Aloud he said:

'Make yourself at home. I'll get the boys to put up a tent for you.'

6 | Hip-hip-hippopotamus

THE largest lawn-mower Roger had ever seen was cutting the grass.

Just outside the camp, a huge mouth as broad as a door, backed up by a body as big as a safari tent, moved along, the great jaws champing the grass clear down to the roots and leaving a bare path four feet wide.

'Crazy!' said Roger, hardly believing his eyes.

At the sound, the monster stopped chewing, raised his head and looked at Roger with huge goggle eyes that seemed to stick out like glass balls from his flat face.

He took a step towards Roger, then stopped as if to think. This queer, two-legged thing was not doing him any harm, so why should he bother with it? He did not fear it. He could take it at one bite. But it was not his idea of good food. He liked grass better.

'Look!' Roger had found his tongue at last. Hal and his father turned. The hippo's ears went up, and his eyes seemed to reach out a little farther.

'Steady,' said Hunt. 'He's not likely to charge unless we give him cause.'

'He has plenty of room for it,' his father said. 'His stomach is eleven feet long – almost as long as he is. I'd say he measures about fourteen feet over all.'

'How much does he weigh?'

'Probably between three and four tons.'

'See him yawn!' cried Roger.

The hippo, perhaps to show his indifference to these creatures, or because he was still quite sleepy, opened his jaws in an enormous yawn. He revealed a great pink cavern four feet wide and four feet deep. Roger could have stepped inside it – but he had no intention of doing so. The yawn was edged with immense teeth. Most of them were grinders, but those in front were canines three feet long.

'Lots of elephants don't have bigger tusks than that,' marvelled Roger. 'Are they as dangerous as they look?'

'They will go through metal. And these tusks are not unusually large. I've seen them four feet long. The upper teeth grind against the lower and that keeps them worn

down. But if an upper canine breaks off, the lower has nothing to stop it from growing. The greatest length of a hippo tusk ever recorded was five feet four inches.'

'Are they any good – those teeth?'

'They're extremely hard, harder than elephant's ivory. For many years they were used to make false human teeth. I suppose a lot of sportsmen who have come over here hunting hippos didn't realize that they had hippo teeth in their own heads.'

'Do museums want hippo heads?'

'They do. That head would bring seven hundred pounds. But we can do about four times as well as that if we deliver a live hippo instead of a dead head. I think the Hamburg Zoo would like this baby.'

'Baby!' exclaimed Hal.

'Yes. He's not full grown. He's still young enough to get used to a zoo and not be homesick for Africa.'

The hippo was still yawning. 'I never saw such a long yawn,' Roger said.

His father agreed. 'Yes, he's the world's biggest yawner. Sometimes when he comes up out of the water and yawns, he throws his head back so far that he topples over backwards. But his yawn can be very useful. When he lies at the bottom of the river he points his head upstream and holds his big mouth open, and sooner or later some fish that are being carried down by the current will find themselves going down his throat.'

The great thick lips were rosy red. 'Wonder what kind of lipstick he uses,' Roger remarked. 'It would take just about a quart for each lip. He must like red. He has it all over him!'

The whole great black hulk was covered with a reddish moisture. 'Naturalists used to say that the hippo sweats

blood,' said Hunt. 'But it's just a red perspiration. The
hippo doesn't like the heat. That's why he likes to spend
most of his time under water. He easily gets sunburned. If
he is out in the sun very much he has to use skin lotion.
The skin lotion he prefers is mud. You wouldn't think a
hide two inches thick would get sunburned – but look at
those big cracks in the back of his neck. He'll fill them
with mud when he gets to the river. Once I caught a young
female hippo that was suffering so badly from sunburn
that we had to give her an injection of forty c.c.s of penicillin. Then we dug a good mud-hole for her to wallow in,
and within a week she was all right.'

Eight white tick-birds sat on the monster's back and
went about picking at the hide. They paid special attention to the wrinkles, in which they could usually be sure of
finding ticks or other biting and burrowing insects. The
hippo never shook off the birds. Even when one flew into
his mouth after a flitting insect, caught it, and settled
down on a great tooth to enjoy it at leisure, the hippo did
not clamp his jaws shut to punish the impertinent bird.

'The tick-birds are the hippo's best friends,' said Hunt.

When the bird had flown away, the great red cave
slowly closed and the mammoth beast again looked suspiciously at the three humans. He snorted, tossed his
head, and waggled his great rear.

'Just trying to scare us,' said Hunt.

'He couldn't catch us anyhow,' said Roger. 'He's too big
and fat and heavy. I could run twice as fast.'

'That's what *you* think,' Hunt said. 'In spite of his
weight, he can gallop as fast as a horse. Besides, bushes
that would stop you cold would mean nothing to him.
He'd go through them like a bulldozer. Never try to race a
hippo.'

The hippo had returned to his job of eating a path and was beginning to move off.

Hal turned to his father. 'How are we going to catch him?'

'To catch him I'd need your help.' He looked at the bandages that covered the ant-jaws holding together the cut on Hal's arm. 'And today I think you'd better just rest.'

'Rest, nothing! The arm is O.K. Doesn't hurt a bit. Let's go after that fellow.'

Seeing that his son was determined, Hunt said, 'Very well – but don't be in a hurry.'

'If we don't hurry he'll be gone.'

'If you do hurry you'll be a goner. He's making for the river. If there's one thing a hippo can't stand, it's anything that gets between him and water. Then he goes wild. He can be as savage as a lion and an elephant rolled into one. Don't forget – hippo means horse and potamus means river. The "river horse" loves water, can't bear being shut off from it. Let him get to the river. We'll follow him with the catching trucks and try to haul him out into a cage.'

The plan was perfect, except for one thing. The three Hunts had forgotten about their guest, Colonel Bigg.

The colonel had gone on a little walk down to the river. For a while the grass was only two or three feet high. As he got down into the lower land, where there was more moisture, the elephant grass grew to a height of fifteen feet. Elephant grass is really a grass, though it looks more like a reed or cane. It is very tough, and has sharp edges. If you brush your way through it, you are sure to be badly scratched. Often it grows so thick that it is impossible to get through – impossible for a man, but the powerful hippo barges through, making a path that other hippos

follow. When many have gone that way, the path is quite
smooth and clear, with a wall of elephant grass rising on
each side and bending to meet overhead, forming a tunnel.

The 'hippo tunnel' is used not only by the hippos but by
many other animals, and man as well.

But when a hippo is passing through the tunnel towards
the river, anything that gets in his way is out of luck. The
hippo does not change his mind easily. When he is set
upon getting to water, he will plunge straight ahead with
open jaws and tackle even a rhino or an elephant that
blocks his way. And as for a mere man-size creature, such
as Colonel Bigg, that would not stop a water-loving river
horse for one moment.

The colonel, enjoying the cool morning air and the
shade beneath the canopy of grass that closed over his
head, was returning from the river. He was thinking about
lunch, although he was still full of breakfast. He was re-
flecting upon what an easy life he had fallen into, thanks
to these suckers who had let him join their camp.

There was a rustling ahead, but he paid no attention to
it. He walked along with his eyes on the ground. The rustling increased, and he looked up. Two huge bulging eyes
stared into his own. Behind them was a great black mass
that completely filled the tunnel from wall to wall.

The hippo stopped and so did the man. The animal
opened its mighty red mouth full of flashing swords and
let out a terrific bellow, a grinding, gritty roar that
sounded like the dumping of a load of gravel.

The colonel fired from the hip and, of course, missed.
The target wasn't quite big enough for him. The sound
further enraged the beast. It came forward at a fast trot,
and the colonel promptly turned tail and ran.

He was not worrying too much. Surely he could run

faster than this clumsy lubber. This great awkward hulk
of fat would never catch him.

A blast of hot air from the big mouth behind him
warmed the back of his neck. He dropped his rifle and
speeded up. But he could not escape those terrific puffs of
hot air. They were like the spurts from a jet engine. One
blew off his hat. The beast snorted as if with savage
pleasure, and the colonel could feel a great lip, or it could
be a tusk, nuzzling against his shoulder.

He stumbled and fell flat. Now the living steam-roller
would go over him. He would be crushed into the ground
by the thousands of pounds of angry fat.

Instead, he felt himself seized by the bush-jacket and
tossed up through the grass roof, sprawling through the
air, then scratching down through sharp-edged elephant
grass to lie at last, gasping and itching, in what seemed
like a bed full of razor-blades. He heard the steam-roller
thunder by, then splash as it plunged into the river.

Bigg crawled out of his uncomfortable nest into the
hippo tunnel. Bloody grass-scratches streaked his face and
hands. He was sure all his bones were broken. He felt
himself all over and could find nothing wrong except that
there were large holes in the back of his jacket, punched
by the brute's teeth.

He staggered up through the tunnel, found his gun, and
picked it up. Then he heard voices and saw John Hunt
and Hal coming from the camp. Bigg pulled himself
together.

'What's up?' said Hunt. 'We heard a shot.'

'Yes,' said Bigg, trying to collect his thoughts. It never
occurred to him to tell just what happened. True to his
nature, he must make a big story of it.

'How did you get bloodied up?' Hal wanted to know.

'Hippo,' said Bigg. 'I met him in the tunnel. We had a fight to the finish. But I got the best of him.'

'But those scratches?'

'Made by his teeth. For a while I was practically in his mouth.'

Hunt said, 'Strange marks to be made by teeth. They look more like grass cuts.'

Bigg looked indignant. 'I hope you don't doubt my word, sir. It was a hand-to-hand struggle, against great odds. A thirteen-stone man against a three-ton beast. Finally I managed to get my gun into his mouth and I nearly blew off the top of his head.'

'So you killed him? Where's the body?'

'Oh, he just managed to get to the water before he died. Probably the body has been washed away downstream.'

Hunt smiled. 'Well, suppose we just go and take a look.'

Bigg blocked the way. 'I tell you it's no use. You want live animals, not dead ones. He's as dead as a doornail.'

A thundering hippo snort came from the direction of the river.

'That doesn't sound like a very dead doornail,' Hunt remarked, as he and Hal brushed by the great hippo-killer and went on towards the river. Bigg, still protesting, followed.

They came out on the river bank and there was the hippo, half in and half out of water. Bigg, still unable to believe that he could not fool these 'tourists', insisted that this must be another animal – the one he had shot must have been carried miles away down-river by this time in the current. But the Hunts recognized this to be the same animal that they had studied so carefully as it passed by the camp. The top of its head was not blown off, in fact there was no sign that a bullet had nicked it anywhere.

'We'll go back and get the trucks,' Hunt said. 'Colonel, you might stay here and keep watch. But mind you, no more shooting. You might make a mistake and hit it this time.'

To get the cars to the river it was necessary for the Africans to hack the hippo path wider with their bush-knives. The largest truck carried a cage eighteen feet long, made of stout two-by-fours reinforced by iron bars.

The young bull hippo was now in deeper water. Only the top of his head was above the surface. He could still hear, see, and breathe, because a hippo's ears, eyes, and nostrils are not on the front and sides of his head, but on top.

If he wished to go completely under water he could do so quite easily. His eyes remained open, but large valves closed his ears and nostrils. Taking a deep breath before going down, he could stay there from six to ten minutes.

'He's really wonderfully made,' John Hunt said. 'Not only can he stay submerged three times as long as the best human diver, but he can walk along the bottom, eating water-weeds as he goes.'

'He doesn't seem too friendly,' Hal said.

'You can't expect an animal that has just been shot at to be friendly.'

The hippo snorted angrily, then opened his great red mouth and let out a bellow that echoed back from the hills like thunder. Colonel Bigg shivered and kept well behind his companions.

The cage truck was backed up to the shore and a ramp placed, up which the animal might be hauled into the cage. A two-inch nylon rope of great tensile stength was made fast to a powerful four-wheel-drive truck directly in front of the cage truck. The loose end of this cable was drawn back through the cage and down to the water, where it was finished off with a loop large enough to go over the hippo's head.

'But how are you going to get the hippo to put his head in the noose?' Roger wondered.

'We'll have to help him do that,' his father said. 'Joro, bring one of those canoes.' He pointed to native boats drawn up on the shore. 'We'll paddle out and take the noose with us.'

The canoe was brought, and the Hunts along with Joro boarded it. This left Colonel Bigg and the rest of the Africans on the bank. The colonel declined an invitation to join the boating party.

'I think I'd better stay here and help get the beast ashore,' he said. 'You can't depend upon these blacks. Always fail you just when you need them.'

The canoe was a heavy thing, fashioned from a single log of ironwood, and its gunwale was only two inches above the water. The occupants must be very careful to keep their balance or the craft would upset.

Hal tapped the thick side of the boat with his paddle. 'There's one good thing about it,' he said. 'Even a hippo's jaws couldn't make much of an impression on this.'

'I wouldn't be too sure,' Hunt said. 'Up at Murchison an annoyed hippo took the rear end of a car in its mouth and crushed it like a nut.'

'He's gone,' cried Roger. The eyes, ears, and nose had sunk out of sight and only a swirl of water remained where they had disappeared.

'He seems to be going towards the other bank,' Hunt said.

'How can you tell?' Roger asked.

'By that line of bubbles. Let's follow him. Not too much noise with your paddles.'

It was several minutes before the hippo broke the surface, snorting and sending up a column of spray like the spout of a whale. He seemed displeased to find the canoe close by. He promptly sank again. This time no bubbles betrayed his position.

7 | Canoe, hippo, and croc

T H E canoe suddenly rose straight up into the air, teetered dangerously for a moment, then slipped off the animal's back and slumped into the water, the splash wetting everyone aboard. Luckily the canoe did not capsize.

'Favourite hippo trick,' Hunt said. 'He'll probably try it again.'

'I never did see his head,' Hal complained, for he was holding the noose, ready to slip it over the quarry at the first opportunity.

Five, ten, fifteen minutes passed with no sign of the hippo.

'He couldn't possibly stay down all that time,' Hunt said. 'He must have walked off down-river. That's strange. I could have sworn he would attack us again, he seemed so angry.'

Roger pointed to some broad water-lily leaves that lay on the surface. 'What's going on there?' The leaves bulged upwards. Something appeared to be hiding beneath them. As the men watched, one leaf slipped, revealing the hippo's nose. How long had he been concealed there, breathing comfortably, awaiting his chance to attack again?

Two other hippos now broke the surface and glared at the canoe with their great goggle eyes. One of them, evidently a mother, carried a baby hippo on her back.

'They're ganging up on us,' Hunt said.

'But I thought hippos were supposed to have mild dispositions,' Hal objected.

'Generally, yes. But not when they're shot at. Not when they're blocked off from water. Not when they're hunted, and not when they have young ones to protect. I don't like this situation a bit.'

But there was one who did seem to like it. Hal noticed that Joro's eyes were shining with an evil light. A sort of snarling smile tightened the African's lips. He seemed even happier when two crocodiles that had been basking on the shore came off and began lazily circling the boat.

'I was afraid of that,' Hunt said. 'Crocs and hippo often work together. The hippos spill the men out of the boat, then the crocs come in for the kill. Look – the lily pads.'

The leaves no longer bulged upwards but lay flat on the surface. The bull hippo had gone under. The line of bubbles showed his progress. He was coming straight for the boat.

'Paddle!' cried Hunt. 'Let's get out of his way.'

Three paddles dug into the water to propel the boat forwards. The fourth paddle, Joro's, also went into action, but in reverse. Powerfully, he was pushing backwards, holding the canoe exactly in the path of the approaching bubbles.

'Joro!' shouted Hal. But before he could say more, the water exploded by the canoe and the bull hippo shot straight up into the air until half of his body was out of the water, then brought his forefeet smashing down upon the canoe. Hal, watching his chance, got the noose over the animal's head just as the capsizing canoe tossed its occupants into the river.

The four struggled to right the canoe. No, only three. Hal observed that Joro was swimming ashore. He could

not understand this. African safari men are not cowards.
But Joro was plainly leaving them in the lurch.

There was no time to think about it. The mother hippo
had dumped her baby on the river bank and had joined
the other two monsters in angry snortings and teeth-clash-
ings, while the two crocodiles, no longer lazy, were swoop-
ing closer to the struggling bodies in the water.

It was the bull hippo who put an end to their efforts to
right the canoe. His great red jaws opened, his huge teeth
glistening in the sunlight closed on the boat, raised it from
the water and shook it as a cat shakes a mouse, then
crushed it as if it had been an egg-shell. The ironwood
canoe, so hard that you couldn't drive a nail into it,

crumpled like paper. Fragments fell to the surface and
drifted off.

Roger struck out for shore, Hal close behind, splashing
to keep off the crocs. Roger looked back. 'Where's Dad?'

Their father was floating face down. They swam back
to him, gripped him by either arm and swam him ashore.

Mali and Toto helped them drag the unconscious man
out of the river and lay him on the sand. John Hunt
opened his eyes to find Hal running his fingers over his
chest to see if any ribs were broken.

'What happened, Dad?'

'The bow. Came down on my back. Knocked me out for
a minute.'

'Are you all right now?'

Hunt tried to move. His face twisted with pain. 'Something wrong back there.'

'We'll get you up to camp right away.'

'Not so fast,' Hunt said. 'First I want to see that fellow safe in his cage. Mali, get going with the forward truck.'

Mali ran to the truck, jumped in, started the engine, and eased the car gently forward. The nylon cable that ran back through the cage to the noose that circled the hippo's neck slowly tightened.

It was going to be quite a pull. Three tons of hippo wanted to go somewhere else. Mali slipped the gears into four-wheel drive.

'Easy does it,' called Hunt. 'Don't choke him. Just persuade him.'

The hippo did not seem to know what to make of it. His enemies had gone, and his anger subsided. Something was around his neck, but it was hardly more annoying than a water-weed. He felt himself slowly drawn across the river. Now and then he struggled and when he did, Mali eased up on the pull. When the struggling stopped, the pull began again. At last the young bull found himself waddling up on to the bank.

Now he faced the ramp slanting up to the open cage on the truck. This was enough to make any animal nervous He began to toss his head and bellow.

'Give him the gun,' said Hunt.

Hal knew what his father meant. He took the syringe-gun from under the driver's seat of the truck. It looked like a pistol but it contained no bullets. Instead, it was loaded with a capsule of curare. This is a medicine that can be deadly if too much is used. But a moderate amount shot into an animal only quiets the beast, makes it sleepy, and easy to manage.

Hal placed the muzzle against the hippo's thigh and pulled the trigger. The hippo snorted with surprise, pulled at his noose, and performed a heavy dance on the beach. Since no one did anything more to him, he soon calmed down and the men waited patiently for the drug to take effect. After ten minutes the bull's head began to droop as if his huge jaws were getting too heavy for him.

'Go ahead, Mali,' said Hunt.

Mali started his truck and the line through the cage drew taut. The animal yielded as if in a trance. Sleepily he gave in to the pull of the cable and with slow steps went up the slight slant of the ramp into the cage. The cage door was quietly closed behind him.

Hunt tried to get up but sank back with a groan. Hal and Roger, with the willing help of the Africans, picked him up, carried him to the forward truck and laid him on the boards. Then both trucks drove through the hippo tunnel back to camp, very slowly so as not to jolt either the disabled man or the caged animal. Hunt was laid on his cot in his tent. Hal bent anxiously over him.

'It's my back,' Hunt said. 'Slipped disc or bunged-up nerves or something – makes all my left side numb.'

'I think I'd better go and get a doctor,' Hal said.

Hunt grinned. 'You talk as if you'd find one just round the corner. I don't need a doctor. I know what he'd tell me to do. He'd tell me to rest – and perhaps have a little massage. Mali can give me that. He's good at it. I'm sorry to poop out on you this way. If I know these back ailments, it may take a week or two for me to get on my feet. During that time, I'm afraid you'll have to go it alone.'

'Don't worry about that, Dad. Give me your order-sheets so that I'll know what animals are wanted – then we'll go and get them.'

'I know you will. I'm not worried about that. But there's something else.'

He closed his eyes. Hal waited. 'What is it?' he said finally.

'I hate to bother you with this,' his father said, 'but it's something you should know. That leopard-man who tried to lead us away from the trail of the leopard last night – I think I know who it was.'

'Someone from the village?'

'No. Someone from our own camp.'

Hal, greatly surprised, objected. 'Now, Dad, that's not possible. None of our men would do that. Besides, we know where every man was. They're all accounted for.'

'Except one,' said Hunt. 'How about Joro?'

'Well, what about him? You told him to go along with us, but he misunderstood. He stayed in camp.'

'The cook tells me he was not in camp last night. This morning, while it was still quite dark, I saw him creep out of the bushes to his tent. Later, I talked with him. He was very nervous. What he said didn't ring true. He seemed to be a man in torture, torn this way and that. I wanted him to tell me what was troubling him, but he would not. I strongly suspect he was the leopard-man.'

'I can't believe it,' Hal said. 'Joro is a fine man, and a wonderful tracker.'

'Agreed. But didn't you notice anything strange when we were trying to get out of the way of that hippo? We were paddling forwards. What was Joro doing?'

'It *was* a bit peculiar,' Hal admitted. 'He seemed to be paddling backwards. Perhaps he thought we stood a better chance of escape if we backed up.'

'I'd like to believe that,' his father said. 'But I'm afraid he was trying to hold the canoe just where it would be struck by the hippo. To put it plainly, it looked as if he wanted us to be dumped and hoped we would be drowned or killed by the hippos, or the crocs, or both.'

'But he was putting himself in danger too.'

'Didn't you see how fast he got himself out of danger? We stayed to try to right the canoe. Did he help us?'

Hal tried to remember. 'Now that I think of it, he didn't. He set out for the shore as fast as he could go.'

'Right. And when we got ashore, he looked angry and disappointed. His plot had failed. But mark my words, he'll try again.'

'But why in the world should he want to kill us?'

'I don't think he does want to. But that's what he's trying to do.'

Hal looked puzzled. 'Dad, your bump must have affected your brain. You contradict yourself. You say he wants to and doesn't want to. Does that make sense?'

'It makes African sense. It makes Leopard Society sense. This isn't London. It's the Dark Continent, and it's still pretty dark, believe me. A couple of dozen African countries have become independent during the last few years, and they have parliaments and presidents and delegates to the United Nations, and they are making a lot of progress and we hope the best for them. But that must not blind us to the fact that outside the cities, away back in these forests, life is just about as savage as it was a hundred years ago. There are still thousands of cannibals in the African jungle. Ninety per cent of black Africans have never been inside a school. They blame everything on the white man. You've heard of the Mau Mau – the secret society that makes its members promise to kill whites. It was at its worst in 1952 but popped up again in 1958, and now it has become more secret than ever and is likely to go on as long as there are white men in East Africa holding land that the blacks think should belong to them. More than twenty thousand people have been killed by this society. Most of the killers don't want to kill – the society makes them.'

'How can they make them want to do what they don't want to do?'

'Simple. They grab a black man and tell him he will be tortured to death unless he takes an oath to kill whites. If he objects, they begin the torture. When he gives in, they make him take an oath to kill, and to make him remember the oath he must eat a dinner of human brains, blood, sheep's eyes, and dirt.'

'And the Leopard Society?'

'Like the Mau Mau, but very much older. The Society seizes a good man and makes a bad man out of him. He must promise to kill. He is given a leopard suit and told he can change into a leopard and must defend all leopards. The heads of the Society are usually witch-doctors. Africans have a deadly fear of witch-doctors and will do anything they tell them to do. If the new member will not promise to kill, he himself and his wife and children are killed. So what can the poor man do? He is caught in a trap.'

'And you think Joro has been pledged to kill us?'

'It certainly looks that way.'

'Then we'd better fire him, at once. I'll take care of it.'

'Not so fast, Hal. As you said, he's a good man and a good tracker. We need him. What's more, he needs us. He needs somebody to get him out of this horrible trap they've got him into. Now I know it's risky to have a man around who's bent on killing us. But we've run risks bigger than that. Now that we know what to look out for, I'm sure we can take care of ourselves. Tell Roger. And both of you, watch your step.'

'But just what do you hope to accomplish?'

'I don't know yet,' Hunt admitted. 'Somehow, a way may open up. In the meantime, carry on with Joro as usual. He must not suspect that we know.'

Hal went out, shaking his head. He respected his father's desire to help Joro. But wasn't it pretty dangerous to try to help a man who was out to murder you?

8 | The colonel dances

HAL counted his troubles.

Some other time he would count his blessings, but just now he was counting his troubles. Number one was his father's accident. Number two was the responsibility that had fallen upon him to take charge of the animal-collecting. Number three was the leopard-man. Number four was Colonel Bigg.

The first thing he saw as he came out of his father's tent was the colonel, posing for a photograph. He had interrupted the men who had been skinning the leopard. The dead animal lay stretched on the grass. Colonel Bigg stood, gun in hand, one foot on the leopard's head. Mali was holding a small camera.

'You are just in time,' the colonel said to Hal. 'Take the camera. Mali is not such a good photographer. It's all set – just get me in the view-finder, then press the trigger.'

'But what's the idea?' asked Hal, quite puzzled.

'Just a picture. Being a White Hunter, I have to have a few pictures. Just to show I can kill leopards and things.'

'But you didn't kill this leopard.'

'What of it? I might have done.'

'But you're claiming credit for something you didn't do.'

'Oh, I see, you're jealous, young man. You killed the leopard and you think you did something great. Why, I've

killed hundreds of leopards, thousands. Just didn't happen
to have a camera with me. Now I have the camera and
here's a leopard, and what does it matter whether it's one
of mine or not? Tell you what I'll do – you take a shot of
me, and I'll take one of you. That way we'll divide the
credit, fifty-fifty. That's fair enough, isn't it?'

Hal laughed. 'Thanks, Colonel. I don't want either the
credit or the photograph. Hold it.' He snapped the picture
and gave the camera back to Colonel Bigg.

Hal walked away, chuckling. He had never met anybody quite like the colonel. The man was harmless
enough, so long as he only wanted his picture taken. But a
fool was a dangerous person to have along on a safari.
This fake White Hunter would have to be watched. He
might get himself and everybody else into serious trouble.

A scream behind him made him turn round. The colonel was already in trouble. He was dancing and prancing,
yelling at the top of his voice, ripping off his jacket, shirt,
and trousers, slapping his body, and stamping his feet.

Hal could guess what had happened. He had seen
soldier ants at work during his Amazon journey. Now
the ants had been attracted by the leopard's carcass, and
when the colonel placed his foot on the animal's head the
ants had swarmed up his legs and were puncturing every
part of his body with red-hot needles.

Hal ran back into camp. He did not run fast enough to
suit the colonel.

'Hurry up! I'm being eaten alive. Do you want 'em to
kill me?'

He was astounded when Hal paid no attention to him.
Hal had something else to think of besides a dancing
colonel.

Soldier ants are one of the greatest terrors of the tropi-

cal jungle. They march across the country like an army
and devour everything in their path. They swarm over
their prey in a thick blanket. They can strip the hide from
an elephant.

'Make fire!' he yelled to the Africans. 'A ring of fire all
round the camp.'

The ants already in the camp were bad enough. But
behind them would be a column of soldiers perhaps a mile
long, marching steadily towards the camp.

The colonel would have to take care of himself. Hal
dashed into his father's tent. If the ants attacked a helpless man he might be killed.

'Ants!' Hal cried.

His father needed only that one word to get the whole
story.

'None here, Hal. The hippo. Quick!'

Hal was out again and racing to the hippo's cage. He
would open the cage door and let the animal escape rather
than allow it to be murdered by the ravenous ants. The
hippo was trembling with fear, for even the largest animals know this danger and dread it. But the ants had not
yet climbed the wheels of the truck. Hal jumped into the
driver's seat, started the engine, and drove the truck
several hunded yards out of camp.

His next thought was for the baby leopards, and the
dog. He came running back to the camp-site, whacking as
he ran the few ants that managed to get on his body.

He found the dog and the spotted kittens huddled together, while Joro thrashed the ground around them with
an old shirt, driving away the ants.

To Hal this was an amazing sight. Here was truly a
man divided against himself. Joro was pledged to be a
murderer. He was ready to kill men. The savage was

strong and fierce within him – yet also inside him was a very gentle heart that prompted him to protect two leopard cubs and a dog.

His own body was not free of the biting ants, but he let them bite as he beat away the danger from the whimpering animals.

Who could hate this good-hearted killer? Hal at last saw clearly that his father was right. Even if it was dangerous to keep Joro, he must he kept and somehow freed from the deadly grip of the Leopard Society.

The ring of fire that the men had made round the camp prevented more ants from coming in, and those already inside were either killed or driven out. The marching army had changed its course to go round the camp and beyond into the jungle. Hal made sure that their path did not take them near the caged hippo.

Now at last he had time to think of the yelping colonel. Bigg had got rid of his last scrap of clothing and was grabbing himself here and there and wherever he felt a new bite. The huge ants, never less than half an inch long, dug their pincers into the flesh and did not relax their hold, even when their entire bodies except the head had been torn away.

The tingling of his own arm reminded Hal of the line of heads that closed his wound beneath the bandage, and he could sympathize a little, not too much, with the cavorting colonel. He pulled out his knife and ran the back of it over Bigg's body, scraping off the heads.

Bigg was not grateful. 'Took you long enough to get to it,' he grumbled. His voice was hoarse from much squawking. He pulled on his clothes. He was still shivering and shaking. Hal turned to the cook.

'Got any coffee?'

'Plenty,' said the cook cheerfully. He had not been bitten, since the ants had kept well away from his fire, so he had been able to attend to his duties as usual. He filled the canteen with strong, hot coffee and passed it to Hal, who poured some of it down Bigg's throat. Hal kept the canteen strapped over his shoulder, in case anyone else needed some of the same medicine.

As Bigg began to feel better, he seemed to expand and grow until he was once more the great White Hunter. He surveyed the camp like a general inspecting his army.

'This would never have happened,' he said, 'if I had been running this safari. All this trouble could easily have been prevented.'

'How?'

'With ant-poison. Surely you have some.'

'I believe there are some boxes of it in the supply wagon,' said Hal. 'It's good for ordinary ants. I don't think it would have stopped the soldiers.'

'You don't think? That's what's wrong with you young fellows, you don't think. This camp is still in danger, you know. Those ants are going round us just now, but they may change their evil little minds at any moment and come straight through the camp. But don't you worry – I'll fix them.'

He went to the van that held the supplies, rummaged about among boxes and packets, and emerged with a tin of ant-poison.

He just wants to show how clever he is, thought Hal. Well, let him have his fun.

Bigg stepped over the burning bunches of grass, twigs, and sticks with which the men had ringed the camp, and began to sift ant-poison on the hurrying ants, taking good care to keep his feet well away from the line of march.

The ant army came on in a column about a foot wide, the soldiers marching so close together that they touched. They did not seem to mind the poison that sifted down upon them like a miniature snow-storm.

Bigg followed the column back to where it emerged from the forest, sifting as he went. He walked on into the woods until he could no longer see the ants because of the thick underbrush.

Then, well satisfied with himself, he returned to camp. The ants, however, kept marching by. For an hour they kept coming. Then the last of them passed and the protecting fires were allowed to die out.

Bigg, his self-conceit completely restored, beamed upon Hal.

'Well, my boy, it's a good thing I thought of the ant poison, isn't it? You see how well it worked. Next time you'll know what to do.'

Hal was about to point out that the poison had not worried the ants in the least. But what was the use of arguing? He would never convince Colonel Bigg. So he smiled and said nothing.

9 | The poisoned baboon

A LOUD clatter of voices came from the woods – shouts, barks, what sounded like the wail of a suffering infant, and high-pitched screams like the voices of women in distress.

Hal stopped to listen. The sounds were almost human, but he knew they came from the large troop of baboons that inhabited the forest. What was bothering them?

He pulled out his father's order-sheets. Baboons – yes, a travelling circus wanted two of them.

Perhaps if he wandered down to the woods and took a look at the troop, he could think out the best way to capture two baboons. Besides, he was curious to find out what was the cause of all this disturbance.

He walked slowly down to the edge of the forest, following the poison trail laid by Colonel Bigg. As he came in under the trees and saw angry baboons in every direction, he realized that he should have brought a gun, or at least some staunch companions, for these brutes were in anything but a good mood.

Everywhere, on the ground, in the branches, the baboons, sometimes called dog-headed monkeys because of their long, dog-like faces, peered angrily down at him. He made a hasty estimate of their number. There must be three hundred of them.

As a naturalist, he had learned enough about baboons

to know that he was in real danger. All the scientific reports on animal behaviour that he had read, and all the hunters he had talked with in Nairobi, agreed that baboons are among the most quick-tempered of animals. At one time they might be as mild as milk, but when they become excited there is no animal more savage.

The big fellows weigh eleven stone, and one of them is a match for a man. Two of them can tear a leopard to bits.

They are more to be feared because they are remarkably intelligent. They react much like human beings. Throw a stone at a baboon and he will throw one back, and his aim is good. He will pick up a stick and use it as a club.

He knows how far an average rifle will shoot and keeps just far enough away to be out of range. He likes to tease the man with the gun. He will put his head down, look at the hunter from between his legs and make faces at him.

Only the birds have sharper eyes. Scientists credit the baboon with eyes equal to eight-power binoculars.

When they make a raid on the farmer's crops, one of them stays up in the top of a tree to act as a sentinel. He gives warning of any approaching danger.

But he knows the difference between a man and a woman. Also the difference between a man with a gun and a man unarmed. He gives a shrill alarm when he sees a gunman, a mild alarm when he sees a man without a gun, no alarm whatever at the appearance of an unarmed woman.

A ranger had told Hal that the baboons knew his car and kept well away from it. When he wanted to approach them closely he had to use another car. Also the baboons recognized the uniforms of the African game-scouts, who are called askaris. When a farmer saw his crops being ruined by animals, he would call the askaris. They would come in, shoot some of the marauders, and scare off the rest.

That would work very well if the animals were rhinos, buffaloes, hippos, wart-hogs, forest pigs, or even elephants.

It didn't work with baboons. As soon as they saw the uniforms, they didn't wait to be shot at. They disappeared as if by magic. When the askaris had gone, they would return and continue their thievery.

To get close enough to shoot them, the askaris must take off their uniforms and put on plain clothes so that they looked like ordinary villagers. And as they walked towards the baboons they must conceal their guns behind their backs.

Even so, a baboon sentinel up a tree might catch sight of a gun and give the alarm, whereupon every baboon would promptly vanish.

The baboon is smart enough to know what is good to eat. He is not like the lion who will eat no grass, the elephant who will eat no meat, the crocodile who will eat no vegetables, the leopard who will eat no shrubbery, or the giraffe who eats only the leaves of trees.

The baboon, like the human being, has learned the value of many different kinds of food. He enjoys fruit, berries, sprouts, vegetables, insects, worms, snails, young birds, and when he is very hungry he may kill and eat pigs, sheep, lambs, goats, chickens, and dogs.

He has one great advantage over man. A man cannot take more food if his stomach is already full. A baboon can. He stores the extra food in his cheek pouches. He keeps it there until there is room for it in his stomach. Then he takes it out of these storage pockets, chews, and swallows it.

A scorpion is dreaded by most animals because of the poisonous stinger at the end of its tail. The intelligent baboon does not worry about that. He knows exactly where the stinger is and how to pinch it off and throw it away. Then he eats the scorpion.

If you let baboons alone they will let you alone. That's a pretty good general rule. But it's not always true. Suppose someone else has made the baboons very angry. Then you happen to come along. They may take out their anger on you.

Hal faced three hundred angry baboons. Certainly he had done nothing to provoke them. Had anyone else annoyed them? Had anyone from the camp been in the woods today?

He could think of no one until his eye happened to rest upon a pale-green dust on the ground. Ant-poison! The blundering Colonel Bigg had been there and left a trail of poison.

But why should that bother the baboons? They were wise enough not to eat poison.

A pitiful wailing like the loud crying of a woman came from a female baboon whose arms wrapped round a screaming baby. Suddenly Hal understood. The small baboon's lips were covered with a pale-green foam.

Not as wise as its elders, it had eaten some of the green poison. Now it was suffering terrible pain. It twisted, writhed and screamed in its agony. Death was not far away.

The troop could not punish Colonel Bigg, but here was a man they *could* kill and they showed every intention of doing so. They bared their great canine teeth, furiously barked and screamed, and danced up and down with rage.

Hal knew that one false move on his part would bring them upon him like an avalanche. If he picked up a stone and threw it, that would seal his own fate.

He stood perfectly still and calculated his chances. If he turned his back on them and ran, they could overtake him.

Perhaps he could quietly withdraw. He took one step backward, then another. He heard baboon voices behind him. He turned and saw that his escape was cut off. The three hundred baboons had so distributed themselves that they completely surrounded him.

Now they were beginning to move in on him and their angry jabbering rose to a high pitch. One by one they would leap forward, then back, then forward again. Each of these cavortings would leave them a little closer to their victim.

Hal gave up any idea of escape. He would try something else. If baboons were so intelligent, he would appeal to their intelligence.

Instead of retreating farther, he took a step forward. The surprised baboons shrank back a little and there was sudden silence.

Quietly, Hal spoke to them. He said anything that came to his mind. It didn't matter what the words were, because they couldn't understand words. But they could understand the tone of his voice. It was gentle and kind, and there was no fear in it.

As he spoke, he looked at the suffering youngster. He loosed the strap from his shoulder and held his canteen out at arm's length. He shook the canteen slightly so that the splash of the liquid could be heard. Then he raised the

canteen to his lips as if to take a drink. Again he stretched
it out towards the baby, all the time speaking gently.

He took another step forward. Immediately the baboon
mother screamed and began to back away. But the
baboons behind her did not let her go.

Three grave, wise old fellows seemed to be reasoning
with her in a sort of conversation made up of low grunts
and barks. They appeared to be saying:

'Perhaps he isn't so bad after all. Perhaps he can help
your baby.'

The mother was hard to convince. She clutched her infant more closely and tried to slip away. When Hal took
two more slow steps forward, she screamed with terror
and that started the baby shrieking once more. Some of
the other man-haters in the troop began roaring anew,
and their savagely bared teeth did not make Hal any more
comfortable.

He stood perfectly still until the noise died down. Then
he spoke soothingly and offered the canteen once more.

It was the baby itself that decided in favour of Hal. It watched him with great round eyes, then reached out its hand towards the canteen. Hal did not move. The baby, straining to clutch the canteen, tried to free itself from its mother's grip. It had the curiosity of any child, the desire to get hold of a strange new thing and play with it.

It began a loud whimpering. The mother, losing patience, turned her brat upside-down and whacked its little red bottom. She tried again to escape, but now she was completely walled in.

Hal had only a few feet more to go. He went down on one knee. Now he did not look quite so terrifying.

Little by little he inched forward. His heart was beating wildly. He was quite aware that this was a dangerous experiment. Perhaps this strong, bitter coffee would counteract the poison. On the other hand, perhaps it would kill the patient. If it did, the 'doctor' would promptly be ripped up into small pieces by three hundred sets of savage teeth.

Suspiciously the baboons watched. How could they be sure that the stuff in this thing was not more poison? But Hal's manner and voice quieted their fears.

Like all animals, they respected courage. If Hal had bolted, they would have been on him in a minute. His easy, steady advance had them puzzled and almost convinced

One last, long reach and the baby had clutched the canteen. Hal did not allow it to be drawn from his hand. He shuffled forward a little closer to his patient in spite of the angry muttering around him. He removed the cap from the canteen.

Then very slowly, he raised the canteen, tipped it, and let a little of the contents drip out.

The baby instinctively opened its mouth to catch the dripping liquid. Hal poured the coffee down its throat. The baby choked and sputtered, then opened its mouth to get more. The rest of the coffee went down the hatch.

Would it kill or cure? The young baboon closed its eyes, then began to twist and cry. The mother was making threatening sounds, other baboons were snarling, and Hal, looking about, could see nothing but row upon row of great yellow teeth crowding in on him.

Hal laid down the canteen. The small baboon suddenly squirmed out of its mother's arms and lay face down on the ground, panting and wheezing. Hal watched every move in an agony of suspense. If the little beast died, he would die too.

Spasms shook the small body, at first in rapid order, then farther and farther apart. Finally the baby lay without movement.

Hal reached beneath and squeezed the baby's belly, hard. Greenish-yellow curds came in a flood from the youngster's mouth. Hal squeezed again and again, until nothing more came out.

Now, still on his knees, he waited. He had done all he knew how to do. It was not a hot day, but he found himself sweating at every pore. The strain had been greater than he realized.

The barking about him had risen to a steady roar. The mother took up her apparently dead baby and began to wail over it.

Suddenly there was a tightening of the small muscles and the little round eyes flickered open.

The barking of the baboons was suddenly hushed. Then there was low chattering, but there was no longer any anger in it. The apes began to amble off into the woods.

Hal, his heart bursting with relief, picked up his canteen and screwed on the top. For another ten minutes he waited as his small patient steadily recovered its strength. Now there were no baboons left in sight except these two, mother and child.

Hal rose slowly to his feet. The mother's yellow-brown eyes looked up at him with an expression of gratitude that would warm the heart of any doctor. The baby was chattering and stretching out its small brown hand for the canteen.

Hal turned and started towards camp. The youngster raised its shrill voice, struggled out of its mother's arms, and pursued the dangling canteen. Its mother gave it a good scolding, ordered it to come back, but when it did not she ambled slowly after it.

So it was that Hal walked into camp with two prize trophies captured only by love and a canteen.

10 | Apes are smart

THE big baboon stopped when she saw the men. Hal took her hand. On the other side he took the hand of the youngster. He strolled in with his two companions as if he were in the habit of going for a walk with apes every day of his life.

The men stood speechless with surprise. Hal enjoyed the sensation he was causing. Now the men would congratulate him on the capture of these two fine specimens.

Then Roger found his tongue.

'What a happy family!' he cried. He opened the flap of the tent where his father lay. 'Dad, you ought to see the three baboons. Papa, mamma, and the baby.'

Hal, grinning at his mischievous brother, took his new friends into the tent.

His father propped himself up on his elbow and carefully examined the big and little apes.

'Perfect. Couldn't be better. But where's the other? Roger said there were three.'

'I'm the other,' Hal said.

John Hunt laughed. 'Roger should be careful how he calls his brother a baboon. That makes him one too. Not to mention me.'

'As a matter of fact,' Hal said, 'I don't mind being called a baboon. They're pretty smart.'

He told the story of his adventure with the three hundred baboons.

'You did well,' his father said. 'And so did they. They showed rare intelligence. They understood you wanted to help the youngster. Few other animals would have acted as wisely. Baboons can be extremely vicious, but they can also be very friendly when they know that they are not going to be harmed. I wonder what goes through a baboon's mind when he sees a man. We look more like himself than any of the other animals, so perhaps he just thinks of us as fellow baboons, only a little bigger and a good deal more stupid, because we can't speak his language and our eyesight and hearing and sense of smell are not as good as his. We can't run as fast, and we can't climb as well as he can. But he must know that there are some things we can do quite well. We can shoot fire out of the end of a stick, and perhaps we can even cure a sick baby.'

'But I never dreamed,' Hal said, 'that an adult baboon would let me bring it into camp.'

'That's not surprising. Baboons often hang around a camp and even run in among the tents and snatch food. They climb up on cars and stick their hands in through the windows, demanding something to eat. They can sometimes make themselves a great nuisance. They get angry easily, but they become affectionate just as easily. If they are in danger from other animals, they may run to the nearest village for protection. Not long ago, when a gang of men were working in Rhodesia, they heard the roar of a lion and the scream of baboons. Then the baboon troop came running out of the bush and nervously squatted along the track as near to the men as they could get. They did not return to the bush until they were sure the lion had gone away.'

'Are they easy to tame?'

'All apes are easily tamed. Of course, some learn more quickly than others. Some are clever, some stupid, just as some people are clever and some stupid. But they can be taught to do many more things than other animals, because they not only have brains, but hands. I wonder if we appreciate our hands. They are marvellous instruments and much of what we do would be impossible without them. Baboons use their hands very skilfully. I'll give you an example. There's a piece of rope. Tie one end of it round the big baboon's neck and the other end to the cot.'

Hal did so. The mother baboon seemed surprised and not too well pleased. She pulled the rope tight and tried to break it. When this didn't work, she sat down, ran her fingers round her neck until she found the knot, and began picking at it. It was a tight knot; yet within a minute she had picked it loose and thrown off the rope.

John Hunt smiled. 'What other animal could do that?'

Somewhat worried by her experience with the rope, the large baboon seized her infant's hand and tried to make off, but Hal hung on to the other small hand.

'I think I'd better slap them into a cage,' he said, 'or they will walk out on us.'

'I don't believe so,' his father said. 'Let them both go, and see what they do.'

The two baboons scampered to the tent opening. When no one chased them, they turned about and looked at Hal with big soulful eyes.

John Hunt laughed. 'You are the best friend they have and they know it. They won't need a cage. You couldn't get rid of them if you tried. If you want to seal the bargain, there are some bananas in that basket in the corner.'

Hal gave each of his guests a banana. The youngster

did not know what to do with it and tried sucking it. Then he saw his mother skilfully peeling her banana, and tried to do the same. He made a rather messy job of it, but finally got rid of the skin.

The two sat contentedly, eating the ripe fruit, never taking their eyes off Hal.

From that moment on, they considered themselves regular members of the safari and specially appointed to wait upon Hal at all times.

He named the little one Bab and the big one Mother Bab. Bab rode on his shoulder. Mother Bab stole everything she could lay her hands on and brought it to Hal as a gift of love. Hal was kept busy returning articles to their proper owners.

Both baboons insisted on sleeping with him – a slightly difficult matter, since the narrow safari cot was not intended for three occupants. But Hal accepted the drawbacks of friendship willingly and only regretted that the day must come when his two devoted companions must be shipped away to join the American circus.

Mother Bab was terrified when she saw the two pet leopards.

Baboons and leopards are mortal enemies. A leopard would rather have monkey-meat than any other dish under the sun. Mother Bab knew this, but little Bab did not. Neither did the small leopards know it, for they had not yet eaten monkey-meat, or meat of any sort.

The leopards were tumbling over each other in a wild game when Bab first saw them. He wanted to join in the fun. He waddled over towards them, in spite of his mother's cries of warning. He made a final jump and landed on top of the two squirming bodies, and all three rolled over on their backs in the grass.

Mother Bab broke into shrill chattering and ran to Hal, looking up into his face, very plainly pleading with him to rescue her child from these horrible monsters. Hal petted the furry head and spoke softly.

'Now don't you worry, Mother Bab.'

The small baboon and the two baby leopards sat up in the grass and looked at each other. It was as if they were waiting to be introduced.

'Roger,' said Hal, 'what do you call your leopards?'

'Well, *chui* is the native word for leopard. One of these is a boy and the other a girl. So I thought I'd call them Chu and Cha.'

'All right, Miss Cha and Mister Chu, kindly allow me to present Mister Bab.'

Bab reached forward as if to shake hands with Cha, but he was really interested only in getting his fingers into that lovely gold-and-black fur. Cha gave his hand a playful swat with her paw, then both she and Chu leaped upon the small baboon and rolled him over and over in the grass.

This was a game that both monkeys and cats understand and love. Mother Bab looked on with big, anxious eyes, but her chattering died down.

'You see,' said Hal. 'It's going to be all right.'

He was not quite so sure that it would be all right when Bab disentangled himself, leaped astride Chu's back and went careering round the camp like a jockey on a race-horse. But Chu took it all in fun, and finally dumped Bab into a pail of water, from which the young ape scrambled and proceeded to use the fur of the two leopards as bath-towels.

Mischief was the chief occupation of the three play-mates and they took special delight in playing tricks on

Colonel Bigg. He was afraid of all three and would wake
up yelling bloody murder when Chu pounced upon him in
bed, or scream when he reached into a box and Cha's
small teeth closed on his fingers. When he dozed off in his
camp chair, his mouth hanging open, Bab, who had seen
the colonel using toothpaste, would squeeze the contents
out of a tube and plaster them over the colonel's teeth.

Bab unfortunately could not read the labels on the
tubes, and the colonel would wake up to find his mouth
full of vaseline or shaving-cream instead of toothpaste.

He woke up in the middle of the night to hear stealthy
movements in the tent. At the same time there was a very
bad smell.

It must be leopards, he thought, although he had not
noticed before that they had an unpleasant odour. He was
afraid to get up and investigate. He buried his head under
the covers.

In the morning he found that his safari boots were
gone. He padded out in his bare feet, looking for them.
Scorpions sometimes wandered through the camp ground,
so when he felt a sharp prick on the sole of his right foot
he thought he had been stung.

Shouting for Hal, he stumbled back into his tent and
threw himself on the cot. When Hal came in, the colonel
was foaming at the mouth.

'I'm dying,' he said. 'A scorpion got me. Bring a shot of
anti-venom, quick.'

Hal, knowing that if it was really a scorpion bite it
could be serious, did not stop to make an examination but
rushed out to get the hypodermic, fill it, and come back on
the run to the perishing colonel.

'Ouch!' gasped the colonel, as the needle plunged into
his thigh. 'You were so long about it, it's probably too late

now. I feel the poison creeping up my legs and into my chest. Pretty soon it will reach my heart.'

'By the way,' said Hal, 'where were you stung?'

'On the bottom of my foot. I feel very faint. I'm afraid I'm going to leave you any minute now.'

Hal studied the soles of the colonel's feet. There should be a small hole made by the scorpion's stinger. But there was nothing – nothing but a slightly brown spot like a tobacco stain.

Hal went out and looked over the ground. He picked up a cigarette butt. It was still burning. He brought it in and showed it to the colonel.

'This is your scorpion,' he said. 'You just stepped on a hot butt. I think you'll live.'

11 | Hyenas like boots

THE colonel recovered with amazing speed. Now that he knew he had suffered only a slight burn, not a poisonous sting, his pains disappeared as if by magic.

Of course, he could not admit his own foolishness. He found a way to put the blame on Hal.

'I should think you'd be red in the face,' he said, 'after a blunder like that. Young man, you must learn to think before you act. Imagine – poking a hole in me with that needle and filling me with snake dope for nothing but a cigarette burn! Scorpion, indeed! Where ever did you get that idea?'

'From you,' Hal reminded him.

'I don't recall saying anything about a scorpion. You must learn to use your head, boy, use your head.'

Hal let it go at that.

Mali came in with the colonel's boots. They looked as if sharp teeth had been chewing on them.

'Are these yours?' Mali inquired. 'We found them just at the edge of the clearing.'

'Of course they're mine, you stupid fellow. Why didn't you find them first thing this morning instead of waiting until now?'

He took the boots and turned them over, examining the tooth-marks. 'Ah-ha, I know exactly what happened. It's those cursed leopards. You let them roam all over the camp. They must have been in here during the night. Now look at the boots – they've almost ruined them.'

'Perhaps it wasn't the leopards,' Hal suggested.

Bigg raised his voice angrily. 'What else could it be? Now let me make this plain, young fellow. Those cubs must be kept in their cage at night. Why, they'll be attacking us in our beds next. In their cage, do you understand? Otherwise I leave this safari. Yes, sir, I'll leave you flat.'

Hal grinned. 'Now, Colonel, you wouldn't do that. What would we do without you?'

'In their cage, is that clear?'

To humour the touchy colonel the leopards were put in their cage when night fell. They didn't like it much, and mewed to get out. Leopards are night animals, and enjoy playing or hunting during the hours of darkness. Chu and Cha were quite unhappy about the whole thing, and Roger sympathized with them.

'Why lock them up just to please that crusty old grouch?'

'If we don't,' Hal said, 'he'll keep on blaming them for what happens. And I have a hunch something more is going to happen.'

'What can happen? The cubs can't get out.'

'I don't believe this was done by the cubs. It must have been a bigger animal.'

'Lion?'

'Who knows? But I know how we can find out. Would you like to stay up with me tonight and keep watch? We might have some fun, and perhaps catch something.'

Roger was more than willing. All other members of the camp turned in. The two boys sat with their backs against a tree and waited.

Roger was much excited. The mysterious jungle was

talking with a hundred tongues.

'What's that?' he kept asking. Hal could not give him all the answers, though he had listened every night and had looked up the cries in his manual.

'I think that boom-boom comes from the hornbill. I know that snort – the wildebeest blasts out air from his lungs through the nostrils. Hear the zebras – there must be a lot of them – chatting like a crowd of people at a cocktail party. The jackal makes that yip-yip. Of course those way-down-deep grunts come from the hippos.'

A roar sounded not far from the camp. 'That's a lion,' Roger said confidently.

'Perhaps, perhaps not. It could have been a hyena.'

'But hyenas laugh. There's one now – what a horrible noise!'

The cry was enough to make the shivers go up and down one's spine. It did sound like a laugh.

'Tee-hee-hee-hee-hee-hee-ha-ha.'

This was followed by a sound that seemed to come from a quite different animal. It started low and rose to end in a high squeal.

'Ooooooo-wee!'

Then there came barks of dogs, yelps of puppies, howls of wolves. Then once more the deep roar of a lion – or so it seemed.

'All made by the same animal,' Hal said. 'The hyena. They're getting closer. I think we're going to have visitors soon now.'

Roger was squirming uncomfortably. 'Weirdest noises I ever heard. They give me the creeps.'

Hal agreed. 'They sound like lost souls. The Africans think they are the spirits of the dead. They think that old men who die can come back as hyenas. Another story is

that witches ride hyenas about all night and make these
horrible cries.'

'Well, whatever they are, do you think they can get into
the colonel's tent? He zipped up the front tight.'

'You can't keep a wild animal out of a tent if it really
wants to get in. Most animals don't want to. The hyena
does, and if he can't squeeze in under the side flaps, he
can easily tear a hole through the canvas with his claws
and teeth. And what teeth! The hyena is said to have the
most powerful jaws of any living mammal. His teeth will
crack the toughest bones.'

'Not the bones of a really big animal, like the rhino?'

'Yes, even those. When lions bring down a rhino, they
eat the flesh but leave the bones. When the lions wander
off with full tummies, the hyenas rush in and crunch those
big bones to bits and swallow them. They chew up the
inch-thick hide as if it were so much paper, and they seem
to find it quite delicious. That's why they like the colonel's
boots. They are made of cow-hide and some of the animal
oils are still in the leather. They eat almost anything. At
the safari lodge in Amboseli they sneak up behind the
cabins, upset the garbage-cans, eat the garbage, and if
there is grease on the inside of the garbage-can they will
almost eat the can itself – at least they crunch it so badly
that it can't be used again. In Tsavo a hunter wounded a
hyena, then dropped his gun and ran. The enraged hyena
took the iron barrel of the gun in its jaws and twisted it
into a useless wreck. Hush! Listen.'

There was a rustling in the bushes just behind the tree.
A bad smell came in on the breeze.

'Hyena,' whispered Hal.

'Smells as if he hadn't brushed his teeth,' whispered
Roger. He lifted the catching-rope that lay in his lap.

'Shall we nab him now? Better get him before he gets us.'

'I don't think he'll bother us. We're not dead enough for him. He likes something very dead and very smelly.'

The dog Zulu, roused from sleep by the sound or the smell, growled softly.

'Quiet, Zu,' Hal warned. 'Your chance will come later.'

A black shadow about the size of a very large dog slunk out into the camp ground. There was no moon, but the light of the bright African stars was enough to reveal the hanging head and the body that sloped from the shoulders down to the tail.

At once the animal was joined by another, just like it. Hal's spirits rose. Perhaps they could catch the two of them. His hand itched to throw a lasso. But first he would give them a chance to pay the colonel a visit. Somehow he must show the colonel that it was not the leopards who had made off with his boots, otherwise the poor little cubs would have to be locked up every night.

The hyenas sneaked over to sniff at the cage that stood near the cook's fireplace. They even walked into the cage. Now, with a quick run, Hal could have reached the cage and slammed the door shut. But he did not move.

If the hyenas knew that two boys were sitting under the tree, they paid no attention to them. Animals bold enough to crawl into a tent inhabited by a man are not easily scared by a couple of boys. They wandered over the camp ground picking up scraps of bread, meat, skin, anything edible.

Coming near the colonel's tent, they stopped and sniffed again. Would they go in or not? The boys held their breath and hoped.

The hyenas walked slowly round the tent, pausing here and there to poke their noses under the canvas side-walls.

In most places the side flaps were tucked under the ground sheet, making entry difficult. But one of the two discovered a slight gap, and by pulling at it with his teeth he drew out the canvas, then flattened himself to the ground and crawled in through the hole. The other followed him.

In a moment they came out again, each holding a dark object in his teeth. Roger gleefully nudged Hal. The dark things were the colonel's boots. The hyenas settled themselves near the fireplace, where the fire had long since gone out, and chewing and smacking noises told the boys that the animals were thoroughly enjoying the colonel's foot-gear.

Hal wondered if the game had gone far enough. Should he act now and save the boots from being completely destroyed? He started up, but a mew from one of the little locked-up leopards changed his mind. No, the colonel should have his lesson.

Besides, it was hardly time yet to try to rope the hyenas. They were still on the alert, looking about constantly,

ready to run at any sign of danger. The longer they were
let alone, the more at home they would feel and the easier
it would be to capture them.

After fifteen minutes of boot-chewing, one of the hyenas
was ready for a little dessert.

The pots and pans that had been used to cook dinner
lay about the fireplace. They had not been washed, for the
cook had been afraid to carry them down to the river in
the dark. The grease of antelope steaks still covered them
and nothing could appeal more to the taste of a hungry
hyena.

The beast licked a heavy iron frying-pan, then picked it
up and bit into it, just as he would have crunched a large
bone. Soon both animals were gnawing away as if iron
and copper were the daintiest of foods. The banging of the
metal containers against the rocks of the fireplace woke
some of the men, and heads began to poke out of tents.

'Now!' said Hal. 'Come on, Zu.'

Both boys and the dog ran forward. The hyenas, still
enjoying their meal, hardly noticed. They woke up to their
danger only when nooses settled over their necks.

With a howl of surprise they tried to break away. Hal
stood firm, but Roger was being dragged towards the
bush. Then Zu went into action. She was an experienced
safari dog and knew exactly what was needed. She ran in
and nipped the heels of the hyena. When the beast turned
towards her, she skipped out of the way. She was not
taking any chances with those grinding teeth. Roger, when
the rope slackened a little, turned his end of it round a bar
of the heavy cage.

The other hyena, unable to escape, turned with a savage
rush upon Hal. Zu lunged again. She knew the dangerous
end of a hyena. She didn't make for its head, but always

for its heels. The hyena, with a howl of pain, turned upon the dog, but never could quite reach her.

The Africans were coming out now, prepared to help. Their help was scarcely needed. Zu was nip-nipping her victims towards the cage. One of them rushed in, perhaps thinking there might be safety there. Zu, like a sheepdog, kept herding the other beast towards the door. Finally it joined the first and Hal, leaping forward, slammed the door shut.

Colonel Bigg came waddling out of his tent in his pyjamas – again in his bare feet.

'What's all the noise about?' he scolded. 'Why can't you let a man sleep? What's going on here? Ouch!' – as he stepped on a sharp pebble. 'Where are my boots?'

'There are your boots,' Hal said, pointing to a sort of black puddle near the fireplace.

The boots looked as if they had gone through a meat-grinder. Heavy teeth had ground and mashed them into a black mush.

'Your leopards did that,' raged the colonel. 'I thought I told you to keep them in their cage. I'll kill those infernal little beasts.' He began searching around through the bushes.

'If it's the leopards you're looking for,' said Hal, 'look over there.'

He turned his flashlight on the leopards' cage.

Inside the cage the two cubs stood on their hind feet with their forepaws clinging to the bars, watching the excitement with big eyes that blinked in the strong light of the electric torch.

'They've been cooped up in there all night,' Hal said. 'Thanks to you.'

'Then what ruined my boots?'

Hal turned the light on the hyenas' cage. The two big spotted beasts, heads hanging, paced angrily back and forth, snarling at anyone who came close to the bars.

'They chewed your boots,' Hal said.

'I don't believe it,' retorted the stubborn colonel. 'Your leopards did it.'

'Do you think those two little cubs could chew up a frying-pan?'

'What kind of question is that? Of course not.'

Hal's light swung to the frying-pan. It was so fantastically twisted, contorted, squeezed, jammed, crumpled, dented, and smushed that it would never again fry a steak over a camp-fire.

'What do you think of that?' asked Hal. 'Could a couple of baby leopards do that?'

'Very well then,' grumpily agreed the colonel, 'the hyenas did it. It's the last damage they'll do. I'll see to that.'

'Where are you going?'

'To get my gun.'

Hal blocked his way. Broad of shoulder and topping six feet, he made the blustering colonel think twice about trying to barge through to his tent. Hal spoke to the angry man as to a child. At this moment the boy nineteen years of age seemed older than the man past fifty.

'You're not going to shoot anything,' Hal said quietly. 'Remember, we're here to take animals alive, not dead. Those hyenas are worth one hundred and seventy pounds apiece to any zoo. If you don't stop firing that gun at everything you see we'll have to take it away from you. Now, go in and go to sleep. Don't worry about the boots – I'll lend you another pair. And as for the leopards, now that you know they didn't have anything to do with this, you can't object if we free them. Roger, let out the cubs.'

Roger flung open the cage door. Chu and Cha tumbled over each other in their eagerness to get out. They gambolled about through the grass, letting out little grunts and yips of delight.

Colonel Bigg, with a good deal of mumbling and muttering, disappeared into his tent.

Hal, followed by Roger, went in to their father's bedside.

'Are you awake, Dad?'

'Of course, Hal. I wouldn't have missed this for the world. Good show.'

'Perhaps I was too rough on the colonel.'

'Not a bit of it. The sooner he knows he's not the boss of this safari, the better for him. Congratulations on getting the two *fisi*.' He used the native Swahili word for hyena.

'Well,' Hal said, 'they're worth money, but I can't say they're very pleasant animals to have around.'

'I know what you mean. The hyena has an unsavoury reputation. He makes frightful sounds and he smells bad. He eats dead bodies. People hold that against him. But has it ever occurred to you that we do the same? We eat nothing live, except perhaps oysters. It's a mighty good thing that the hyenas do eat up the dead animals. The wild-animal population of East Africa runs into millions, and every day hundreds of them die for one reason or another. Suppose all those bodies were left to rot, what a stinking jungle this would be! The hyenas are the sanitary squad. They go around and clean things up. They, along with the jackals and the vultures, are the jungle scavengers. We couldn't do without them. Suppose a lion kills a zebra – he eats only part of it, then wanders off. In come the hyenas and eat the bones. Then along come the jackals and eat the scraps of flesh lying about. Finally the vultures arrive and take whatever is left, even gobbling up the bloody sand, so that when they are all done you would never know an animal had been killed on that spot. That's a pretty good clean-up job.'

'They may be useful,' Roger admitted. 'But they look so mean.'

'They do, indeed. But perhaps they're like a lot of people – not as mean as they look. On my last trip to Africa, I saw a hyena run into a camp and pick up a scrap and disappear with it into the bushes. In a moment he came back, got another bit, and off he went with it. This was repeated many times. I got curious and followed him back into the bush. There I found his mate nursing her young, and in front of her were all the scraps. The male had brought them all to her without taking one for himself. And you'd be surprised what nice pets hyena pups can be. They don't have the smell of the older animals, and they are full of fun and as affectionate as dogs. That's natural because they are a kind of dog, you know. Part cat and part dog, but more dog than cat.'

12 | The witch-doctor

DAWN was beginning to grey the walls of the tent. The flaps opened and the gun-bearer Toto looked in.

'May I speak, *bwana*?'

'Come in, Toto. What's on your mind?'

'The little leopard – Chu – the male – he is gone.'

'Probably just running around in the bushes somewhere,' Hal said.

'No, I saw a man take him and run. A man from the village. I chased him but could not catch him.'

'Why should they steal Chu?'

'I think I know why, *bwana*. Last night I was in the village. The headman is sick unto death. The witch-doctor said only one thing could cure him. A goat must be sacrificed. It must be burned alive in front of the headman's house. The men caught a black goat and tied it to a stake and piled much wood around it. They set fire to the wood. The witch-doctor danced around the fire. The goat cried very loudly. The fire burned its legs and then its body, and it died. The witch-doctor took some of the hot ashes and mixed them with juice squeezed from the body of a toad and made the headman drink.'

'Then what?' John Hunt asked. 'Did the chief feel better?'

'No, he did not. He closed his eyes. His face showed his great pain. His body became as stiff as the trunk of a tree. His son said if he died the witch-doctor must also die.'

'That must have frightened the witch-doctor.'

'He was much afraid. He told the people it was their own fault that the medicine had not worked. It was because they did not believe. They did not have enough faith. They had not sacrificed enough. It was too easy to get a goat – they must do something more difficult. And he gave them something very hard to do.'

'What was that?'

'Their headman was no ordinary man, he said, he was their great chief, and a great man must have a great sacrifice. They must feed him the heart of a leopard. Then he would be well. If they did not give him the heart of a leopard within twelve hours, he would die.'

'He was asking the impossible. Leopards cannot be found so easily. It might take them days or weeks to find a leopard.'

'It is so,' Toto said. 'The witch-doctor gave them this hard thing to do and hoped they could not do it. He thought the chief would die. Then the people could not blame the witch-doctor. He could say, "I told you what to do and you didn't do it. If you had brought me a leopard within twelve hours, I could have cured your chief. His death is your own fault." The men turned one to the other in long palaver. Though they talked much, no one could say where they might catch a leopard. And I, weary of much listening, came back to camp.'

'I can guess what happened then,' said John Hunt. 'Someone must have remembered that we had two leopards here in camp. So one of the men sneaked down and waited his chance, and after the cubs were let out he grabbed Chu.'

Roger leaped to his feet. Already the witch-doctor's knife might be cutting out the heart of little Chu.

'Let's get up there in a hurry.'

Hal rose. 'Wait, Hal,' his father said. 'Take the medicine kit with you.'

Hal seized the kit, and the two boys and Toto started on the run up the hill to the village.

They heard the beating of wooden drums, shouting of men, chattering of women. The villagers must be highly excited. Above all this noise rose the howling of a single voice, probably that of the witch-doctor as he worked himself up into a frenzy in preparation for the sacrifice.

The three burst through the ring of huts. They had not arrived a moment too soon.

There was little Chu, standing on his hind feet, strapped to a post by his neck and his heels, his chest exposed ready for the knife. His little forepaws waved helplessly in the air. He was mewing pitifully.

Before him danced the witch-doctor. His body and face were painted in many colours. Strapped to his forehead was a pair of antelope horns. Tall egret feathers and ostrich plumes rose from his hair and waved wildly as he leaped about. A lion's mane had been strapped to his chin so that it looked like an enormous beard.

Hanging from his neck by a cord was a tin can with crocodile teeth dangling in front of it. Every move of his body made the teeth crash against the can, keeping up an unearthly din.

Around his throat was a necklace of hyenas' claws. His only clothing was a strip of giraffe skin round his loins. His bare legs and bare trunk were oiled with crocodile fat and he smelt to high heaven.

As he leaped, stooped, twisted, and yelled, the long

knife in his hand flashed in the sun, and at every sweep its savage point came closer to the frightened leopard.

Around these two central figures danced the people of the village, chanting, praying, shouting, while drummers behind them pounded on hollow logs.

Roger, seeing his pet in danger, did not stop to think of his own safety. He plunged in through the circle of dancers, jerked out his hunting-knife, cut the cords binding Chu, and gathered the whimpering leopard in his arms.

Hal and Toto were at once beside him. The noise stopped abruptly. The people stared in astonishment, their mouths hanging open. They waited for the witch-doctor to strike these impertinent strangers dead.

The witch-doctor himself glared at them with a look of savage hate. He had to look up to meet Hal's eyes, for the

boy was taller than he by a good twelve inches. But he had a knife, and Hal was unarmed. The witch-doctor screamed with fury and raised his knife. Hal seized his arm, gave it a sharp twist, and the knife fell to the ground.

'I want to see your chief,' Hal said.

The wizard looked blank, understanding no English. Toto translated into Swahili. The witch-doctor replied angrily.

'He says you can't see the chief. The chief is very ill.'

Hal looked about. One hut was larger than the others. That would be the chief's home. He pressed through the crowd and entered the open door of the hut. Toto was close behind him, and Roger with the leopard in his arms. The witch-doctor and the villagers followed, and the hut was suddenly full.

On a straw pallet lay the chief. He raised his hand in a weak gesture of greeting.

'My friend,' he said in English.

'If we are friends,' Hal replied, 'why did you let them steal our leopard?'

'It was his plan,' the chief said, glancing at the witch-doctor, 'not mine. I knew nothing of it until they brought the leopard to the village. It should not have been done. We remember that you killed the man-eater that was killing our children. We are grateful.'

'It was a strange way to show gratitude,' Hal said.

'That is true,' the headman admitted. 'But my people are not so bad as you think. They wanted to save my life. That feeling was greater than their gratitude.'

'They were about to kill our pet.'

'I tried to stop them. But a chief's word is not strong when he is near death. Then the witch-doctor takes the power. Perhaps I did not try hard enough to stop them.

After all, I wanted to live. Perhaps our witch-doctor is right. Perhaps eating the heart of an animal that grows strong will make me grow strong. You are a good man. You would not want me to die if I could be saved by the death of an animal.'

Hal smiled and pressed the chief's hand.

'Of course I don't want you to die. But how can you believe this nonsense? How could a leopard's heart help you? You are educated. You know the new things, you even speak English. And yet you give in to this foolish old superstition.'

The chief closed his eyes and said gently, 'Not all the old things are wrong. Not all the new things are true. You also have superstitions.'

Hal felt like a small boy being gently reproved by his father.

'Indeed we do have our superstitions,' he said. 'We have much to learn, and we can learn a great deal from the people of Africa. Still – I *might* have something in this black box that would help you.'

'What is that?'

'A medicine kit. I'm no doctor – but we often have to doctor each other on these trips. You seem to have a fever. May I take your temperature?'

A slight nod was his only answer. But when he opened the kit and took out the thermometer, the witch-doctor began to jabber violently.

'He says,' Toto translated, 'that he knows this thing. It is full of poison and will kill the chief.'

The headman spoke sharply to the witch-doctor, then took the thermometer and put it into his own mouth.

Hal took out his handkerchief and wiped the sweat from the headman's face. He put his fingers on the sick man's pulse, watching the second hand of his watch. When he removed the thermometer and looked at the reading, he said:

'No wonder you feel uncomfortable with a temperature of 103 and a ninety pulse. How long has this been going on?'

'Since midnight.'

'And before that?'

'Headache. Chills. Shivering. I thought I would shake apart. They told me the air was warm, but to me it was icy cold.'

'And your appetite?'

The chief turned his head away with a disgusted expression on his face.

'I cannot bear the thought of eating. That is what sickened me most – the idea of swallowing the bloody heart of the leopard. I am sure it would rise again at once.'

'Do you have pain?'

'Everywhere. In every joint, every bone. I could not say where there is pain, for there is no place where it is not.'

'It sounds to me,' Hal said, 'like an acute attack of malaria.'

He took a medical booklet from his kit and turned to malaria. Then he explored the contents of the black box and picked out two bottles, one marked paludrine and the other quinine. He removed one tablet of the first drug, two of the other. He turned to the witch-doctor.

'Will you bring me a little water?'

The wizard angrily refused. Toto slipped out to the village well and returned with water in an ostrich shell. The chief willingly took the tablets and washed them down.

He paid no attention to the excited protests of his witch-doctor.

'Now, try to sleep,' Hal said. 'In a few hours I'll be back. I expect you to be much better.'

'But if I am worse, my people will make you suffer. I think you had better not come back.'

'I'll be back,' Hal said, and rose to leave the hut.

The witch-doctor suddenly lunged forward and jerked the leopard from Roger's arms. Roger struggled to get it back.

'Leave it alone,' Hal said sharply. 'There are only three of us. Do you want to get into a fight with forty men? What's the witch-doctor saying, Toto?'

'He says he will keep the leopard. If the chief recovers, the leopard will be returned to us. If the chief does not recover, the leopard will be killed.'

Worried about his pet, Roger took it out on Hal. 'Are you going to let them get away with this? What a milksop you've turned out to be! You know they'll cut that cat into little pieces as soon as we get out of the village. Why don't you do something?'

'Come on, you little hothead,' Hal replied, 'before you get us into real trouble.'

The two brothers and Toto started down the hill. A stone caught Hal squarely between the shoulder-blades. The pain made him wince, but he did not turn round. Roger, who had often seen his elder brother's courage, could not understand him now. Hal only said:

'Better a stone than a poisoned arrow. Really, I don't blame them. They're worried about their chief.'

'Well they have a nasty way of showing it,' Roger growled.

At noon the three returned to the village. Men, women, and children ran out to meet them with smiles and friendly chatter.

'He must be better,' Hal guessed.

The chief was still lying down, but his eyes were bright and his greeting was warm. 'I'm all right,' he said. 'Just weak.'

Hal found that his temperature had dropped four degrees, his pulse was normal, the chills and the aches were gone.

Roger was looking anxiously about.

'Bring in the boy's leopard,' the chief ordered. A man fetched the small animal and put it into Roger's arms.

Everybody seemed very happy – nearly everybody. The only sour puss left was the witch-doctor.

It was a bad day for him. His people were laughing at him. His magic had failed. The sacrifice of a goat had not cured the chief. He had failed to take the heart of the leopard. Two boys had stopped him. The high and mighty witch-doctor, stopped by two boys! And one of these boys had cured the chief!

But the witch-doctor was not done. He was raving and ranting to everyone who would listen.

'What is he saying?' Hal asked Toto.

'He says the chief is not cured. He says this is only the last flash of life before death, just as a star is brightest before it drops out of sight. He tells the people that the chief will die. You have poisoned him with the small white things you put in his mouth. And the glass tube you gave him to suck...'

'The thermometer?'

'Yes. It had something red in it. He says it was a deadly poison. It is a poison that makes a man feel better just before he dies. But the chief will surely die. And the spirits will punish all in the village because they did not trust their witch-doctor. So he tells the people.'

'Do they believe him?'

'Their minds are divided. They are happy that the chief is better. But if he dies they will believe you murdered him. They will believe their witch-doctor was right, and he will once more be great in their eyes.'

'And I will be very small.'

'You will be nothing. They will kill you as they would kill a rat.'

'That's what I like about you, Toto,' Hal said. 'You make everything sound so jolly.'

He gave his patient another tablet of paludrine and two of quinine. There was a disturbance at the door and Mali came pushing through the crowd. Breathless from his run up the hill from the camp, he could only gasp:

'*Bwana* ... buffalo ... many!'

Hal did not need to know more. For days he had been watching for buffalo. Three were wanted by the London Zoo. He made his apologies to the chief.

'You will forgive me if I leave at once. But I will come back to see if you are still improving.'

'Thank you, my son.' The words, and the smile that went with them, repaid Hal for all his trouble.

As the three made their way to the door, the witch-doctor's voice rose shrill and harsh above the talk of the crowd. Toto interpreted his words.

'The chief will die. The chief will die.'

'I suppose nothing would please him more,' Hal remarked.

13 | Charge of the heavy brigade

FROM the hill they saw the buffalo. There were about a hundred of the big black beasts.

They looked like a hundred thunder-clouds. They didn't seem to belong in this land of warmth and sunshine. They could start a storm that would be worse than any that could come out of the sky. They looked as if they were aching to do just that.

The entire herd was turned in one direction, facing the Hunt camp. They didn't seem to like what they saw. An African buffalo never seems to like anything. An elephant or a lion or even a hyena has his pleasant moments, but a buffalo always looks as if he had got out of bed the wrong side. His angry red eyes glare out of an ugly, inky-black face, and he stands with his head stretched forward as if trying to reach you with those spear-pointed horns. They are the toughest and stubbornest horns worn by any beast in Africa. A big bull will measure four feet from the tip of one horn to the tip of the other. And he has a ton on four feet ready to push those horns through anything that doesn't please him.

'If they take a notion to hit the camp,' Hal said, 'they'll flatten those tents as if a steam-roller had gone over them.'

The thought that their father, helpless on his cot, would not be able to escape such a stampede took the boys on the run down the hill.

They found the camp busy preparing for the battle with the thunder-clouds on four legs. The men were busy revving up the motors of the trucks. A take-'em-alive safari, if it hopes to catch and carry many large animals, must be well equipped with cars, and there were fourteen in the Hunt outfit.

Not one of them was anything like the family car seen in city streets. They were heavy trucks and lorries, made heavier by metal rods and plates to enable them to stand the terrific banging over rocks, into holes, over ant-hills, and hummocks.

The lightest of them were the heavy, solid Land-Rovers, armour-plated like army tanks and equipped with four-wheel drive to get them out of bad bogs or deep sand. Then there were the stout Ford and Chev 'catchers', intended for chasing the big animals, and the big four-ton Bedfords and Land-Rovers, each carrying one or several huge crates or cages, in which the animals would be placed after they were nabbed by the catchers.

'Our first job is to protect the camp,' Hal said. He ordered the men to drive the cars up into position facing the buffalo. There they lined up with the camp behind them. In front of them, some five hundred yards away, was the black herd. The two armies, one of metal and the other of muscle, glowered at each other.

Hal dashed into his father's tent to report on what he had done.

'That's fine,' John Hunt said. 'That ought to make them think twice. Trouble is, most of them leave the thinking to the big bulls in the front row. If just one of those bulls takes a notion to charge, all the rest will follow, like sheep. But that's the only way they're like sheep. They can be mighty mean. If they start to charge, there is only one thing to do – charge back.'

Hal ran out to instruct the men.

'If they start coming, go to meet them!'

The fourteen drivers kept their motors going. Hal hurriedly appointed others to climb aboard certain of the trucks, so that they would be on hand to help when the time came for the catching and caging.

He did not forget that the whole safari numbered only thirty men, and he must leave enough of them in camp to defend it in case there was a surprise attack. For he knew the reputation of the buffalo – these beasts are as smart as they are mean. If they cannot attack you in front, they have the unpleasant habit of sneaking round and coming up on you from behind. Many hunters regard them as the most dangerous big game in Africa.

The elephant is larger, but sometimes sweet-tempered. The buffalo doesn't know what sweet temper is. Some big game, such as the rhino, cannot see very well, some cannot hear very well, some cannot smell very well. The buffalo can see, hear, and smell perfectly.

You can dodge some animals. You can't dodge a buffalo, because he is quick on his feet and will turn when you turn.

If another big animal gets you down and you play dead, he may wander away. Not so the buffalo. He isn't satisfied to have you merely dead, he wants you flat. He will trample upon you until you are as thin as a French pancake.

Roger, unwilling to be left in camp, boarded a Powerwagon. Hal jumped in beside the driver of a Ford catcher. He was not too happy to discover that the driver was Joro, the man who had sworn to kill him. But there was no time now to think of such matters.

Over the coal-black bodies of the buffalo floated snow-white egrets. Some of them perched on the broad backs, plucking out insects from the cracks in the hide. Most of them circled in the air, sharing the excitement of the animals below them.

The lovely birds, whose feathers are prized for their beauty, contrasted oddly with the ugly monsters beneath them. Here was certainly a case of beauty and the beast. The black army seemed to be waving white flags.

Usually the white flag means surrender, but it was not so this time. Pawing the ground and snorting defiantly, the buffalo had no idea of giving up or running away.

Buffalo fear only two enemies. One is the lion, the other is the gun. They did not see either lions or guns, so why should they be afraid?

They saw men. A man has no horns, and it would take a dozen men to equal a buffalo in weight and more than that to match his strength.

Hal had hoped the buffalo would be worried by the line-up of cars. But to a buffalo's eyes perhaps these things looked like houses or tents, nothing to be afraid of. And Hal himself was not so sure of victory when it occurred to him that this was going to be a contest between about thirty tons of car against a hundred tons of buffalo.

But how about noise? Many creatures were sensitive to noise. Hal put his hand on the horn-button and held it there. The drivers of the other cars got the idea, and four-teen powerful horns let out a roar that sent up the egrets in a white cloud and started the baboons down by the river chattering with terror.

Instead of turning tail, the buffalo set up a tremendous bellowing that quite drowned the sound of the horns.

They howled back at the noise as a dog may howl at music. The horn-blowers gave up. The deep-voiced choir continued for a few moments, then it also fell silent.

A few of the bulls in the front line began to lose interest in the show. They started to graze on the sweet grass They no longer faced forwards like an army about to march. Some turned broadside, and Hal began to hope that the danger of a charge was over.

Then who should run out in front of the cars but the crazy colonel! He was carrying his ·470. Hal remembered that Bigg had said he wanted a buffalo head. Now he saw his chance to get one. Hal shouted:

'Bigg! Don't shoot! Come back!'

Bigg paid no attention. He raised his gun and levelled it on a huge bull, one of the leaders.

Hal leaped from the truck and ran. Before he could reach Bigg, the gun fired. Bigg turned in time to receive a smashing blow in the face from Hal's fist. The gun flew from his hands and he fell in a heap.

The herd began to bellow again, but this time they were not singing to the music of a car-horn orchestra. The bulls were roaring with rage, the cows were making loud snorts of alarm, the calves were mooing and running to their mothers for protection.

The bull that had been the colonel's target was far from dead. The bullet had torn open his forehead. The thickness of the bone had prevented it from reaching the brain. The colonel had accomplished just one thing. He had turned this animal into a devil. An animal that had been only curious was now furious. A wounded buffalo thinks only of revenge.

The bellowing bull tossed his head, flinging a spray of blood into the air from his wound, and then came on like a runaway locomotive, straight for Colonel Bigg.

A moment before, there had been a good chance that the whole herd would start grazing and walk away. Now that chance was gone. The wounded bull had not taken two strides before every adult animal in the herd was on the move. On they came, a bellowing wave of black fury.

Hal, back in the truck, nudged Joro. The car leaped forward, and so did every other car at almost the same instant. They moved just in time to save Colonel Bigg from being trampled to death by the animal he had wounded. They shot past him and closed in so that the bull could not reach him. He dizzily picked himself up, got his gun, and staggered back to camp.

Meanwhile the black avalanche he had started came on and the pounding hooves made the earth shake. The animals in the front row could not have stopped now if they had wanted to. Those behind pushed them on. Dust rose in great clouds and through the clouds screamed the white birds.

The buffalo did not seem in the least terrified by the fourteen iron monsters roaring in to meet them. The drivers did not try to go round rocks and ridges. The trucks bounced and leaped like bucking broncos.

Roger found himself half the time in the air. At every bounce he went up and down like a jack-in-the-box. He was whanged at both ends, his head against the roof, his rear against the hard seat.

Then the two armies met. Such a roaring of motors and bellowing of buffalo and excited shrieking of baboons and birds and all other creatures within earshot surely could never have been heard before in this quiet river valley.

Heavy heads crashed into radiators, bent and twisted the metal, broke open the coils, spilled the water, and brought the cars to a shuddering halt. The horns of a buffalo join on the forehead in a boss of solid bone four inches thick, giving him a terrific battering-ram. Fenders were crumpled as if they had been cardboard, bumpers were broken, headlights smashed.

The shock of the collision threw men forward out of their seats against the windscreens, and one windscreen was struck even harder from the outside when a bull making a mighty leap landed on the bonnet and his great helmet of bone smashed the glass.

Four bulls concentrating on one truck pushed it backwards, slewed it sideways and toppled it upside-down. The car did not burst into flames. The quick-thinking

African driver, when he saw the four black bulldozers about to crash into his vehicle, had turned off the ignition.

Vultures streamed down out of the sky. They always appeared as if by magic whenever there seemed a promise of death.

Here there was more than a promise. No man had been killed, but three of the animals lay motionless, blood streaming from their wounds. Their rock-hard heads had not suffered, but their necks or flanks had been gouged by their metal enemies. They would never again test their strength against a truck. Others, lying stunned for a while, got unsteadily to their feet. They shook their heads, rolled their eyes, but could not make up their minds to charge again. They turned to go. The rest of the herd hesitated.

The drivers of all cars able to move were watching Hal's car, for he was their leader.

'Go ahead – slowly,' Hal told Joro. The truck inched forward. The others did the same.

It was just enough to discourage the buffalo from further attack. One after another the big brutes turned tail and began to trot away.

14 | Buffalo hunt

THIS was the end of the battle. But not the end of the war.

The real job was still to be done. Three buffalo must be caught and caged.

Hal shouted instructions to the drivers of the trucks on either side, and they passed the word down the line. All trucks were to return to camp except two – Hal's Ford Catcher and the Powerwagon carrying Roger. Hal knew this his brother would want to be in on the chase. Operators of the other cars must stand ready to drive out at once if their help was needed. Hal called some of the extra men to ride in the rear of Roger's truck and his own.

Hal slipped out into the catcher's chair. This is a small seat *outside* the cab. It is strapped to the right front fender. The man who is to do the catching must sit in this chair.

He holds a long pole with a noose at the end. The idea is to get the noose over the head of the running animal, but this is more easily said than done.

Hal signalled Joro, and the truck set out in pursuit of the herd. At every jolt Hal thought he would be thrown out of the seat into a thorn-bush. He hung on like grim death with one hand, clutching the pole with the other.

The long grass looked as smooth as velvet, but it concealed pot-holes made by the rain, pits made by burrowing animals, boulders, stumps, and logs.

Now they were actually in the herd. Like a black river, it flowed along on both sides of the car. Some of the animals were within reach of the catching pole, but Hal ignored them. He wouldn't be satisfied with just any buffalo. He wanted one of the big bulls.

Ahead, he saw one, taller by a good eighteen inches than any of the animals around him. His back was as broad as a dining-room table. From his great head the horns swept out and up, ending in points as sharp as icepicks. On the nape of his neck an egret was taking a dizzy ride.

Over the thunder of hooves and the roar of the car, Hal shouted:

'Let's get that one.'

Joro could scarcely hear him, but he understood the pointing finger and speeded up the car. The bumper nudged the rears of some lumbering cows and they veered out of the way, leaving a fairly clear path ahead. Clear, but not smooth. The greater the speed, the rougher the ride.

It would be a miracle if the wildly leaping car did not tear out its sump on a stump or wind up against a rock with a broken axle.

A large acacia tree blocked the path. Joro threw the wheel over, the swerve nearly tossing Hal out of his seat. They barely missed striking the trunk of the tree. Joro did not turn for bushes. He ploughed straight through them. The worst were the thorn-bushes. They stood some fifteen feet high and as broad as the car, and they bristled with thousands upon thousands of thorns, each two inches long and as sharp as needles.

They did not merely scratch Hal's face and hands. They

tore holes in his shirt and trousers and bloodied him from head to foot.

For a moment he wondered if Joro was giving him this treatment on purpose. But he realised that there was no help for it. If they were to catch the big bull they could not stop for bushes.

Nor even for ant-hills. The African ant-hill is a strange and wondrous thing. It may be anything from two feet to twenty feet high. Though called an ant-hill, it is really built by termites, millions of them, and every particle of the hill has passed through the body of a termite. On the way through, the clay is mixed with certain body-juices which turn it into a kind of cement.

So the ant-hill is as hard as rock, and if you attack it with a pick, all you get is sparks. It defies sun and rain and may last more than a hundred years.

It was up the slope of one of these ant-hills that the big bull rushed until he was twice as high as the roof of the car. Hal would long remember that great black body high against the blue sky. Then, instead of running down the other side, the bull leaped into space, trusting to his sturdy legs to give him safe landing.

The truck would lose valuable time if it tried to go round the hill. Joro gave the engine the last squirt of power. The truck shot up like a rocket to the top of the hill. Then it left the earth entirely and took off into space. With bad luck, it could land upside-down. But with good luck, if you would call it that, it crashed down, right side up, into the worst thorn-bush yet.

Porcupine quills growing on bushes, Hal thought as he added to his collection of scratches.

The car ripped its way through the thorns and was once more in the open, now close to the big bull. It was too

close for comfort, and the buffalo increased his speed. His hide glistened with sweat, and foam dripped from his mouth. Now both he and the truck had left most of the herd behind. The bumper of the car almost touched his flying heels. The pole extended over his back and the noose dangled above his head.

Hal tried to settle the noose in place, but succeeded only in bumping the animal's back with his pole. The egret flew up with a sharp cry of alarm. The buffalo wheeled about and went off to the right. Joro at once turned in pursuit, and the car went round the curve on two wheels.

Again it drew close. Again the bull tried to throw it off by a sharp turn, this time to the left. The heavy truck spun about and followed.

Suddenly the bull stopped dead and glared at the truck with savage red eyes. He was tired of being pestered by this smelly monster of metal and rubber.

Joro stopped the truck. The buffalo was now on Hal's side of the car. Before Hal could get the pole and noose into position, the beast charged.

If he had struck the car low down, it would have gone over in a flash, pinning Hal underneath. Instead, he crashed into the door, horns first. He pierced the door as if it had been cardboard.

He found himself locked to this strange, evil thing. He wrenched his head violently, and in doing so not only pulled his horns free but jerked open the door.

Now he could see a human being inside and his fury was redoubled. He reared up on his hind feet and thrust his head and shoulders into the cab.

But Joro was not waiting for him. There was a hatch in the roof of the catcher and it was open.

Even as the great head plunged into the cab, Joro was scrambling through the hatch and on to the roof. He was quick, but not quick enough to escape one horn, which poked him in the rear and speeded him on his way.

Hal and the men in the back of the truck could not help laughing at the way Joro shot up through that hole like a living cannon-ball.

But what happened then was still more amusing, though a bit terrifying. The head of the buffalo burst up through the hatch. By drawing his hind feet into the cab, he even managed to get his forefeet on to the roof.

He was mad with rage, determined that his enemy should not escape him. He swept the roof with his horns, and Joro could barely keep out of his way. The animal

bellowed furiously and flung the spume from his foaming
mouth. His eyes were like burning coals. He struggled
desperately, but could not climb higher through the hatch.

In the meantime his hind quarters and hooves were
working havoc in the cab, battering the metal fittings,
slashing the instrument board and smashing the windscreen.

Hal wished he had a camera instead of a catching-pole.
What a sight this was! A Ford truck with a bull buffalo in
the driver's seat!

Game-wardens had told him of incidents like this –
buffalo, rhino, lion, leopard, bursting their way into cars.
And in America's Yellowstone Park not a year went by
without a report of a black bear or a grizzly breaking into
a car. But it was one thing to hear about it and another to
see it with his own eyes.

He was so entertained that he almost forgot to act.
Then he suddenly woke up. Here was the best chance he
could possibly ask for to catch a magnificent bull.

He swung his pole about until the noose was above the
animal's head. This new annoyance, fluttering above like
a bird, did not improve the buffalo's temper. He roared at
it, tried to stab it with his ice-picks.

Hal opened the noose with a twist on the pole and
lowered it. That should have dropped the loop neatly over
the animal's head. But the rope caught on one of the wide-
spreading horns. A part of the loop fell into the buffalo's
mouth and he set out to destroy it with his powerful jaws.
But a buffalo fights with his horns and hooves, not often
with his teeth. His teeth are meant for grass-eating. The
tough nylon cord resisted all attempts to turn it into chew-
ing-gum.

With a sudden jerk Hal managed to pull the rope loose.

The buffalo had given up trying to reach Joro. He had drawn one of his forefeet down into the cab. Soon he might withdraw his head, then back out of the car and escape. Hal realized he had only one more chance.

As skilfully as he knew how, he manipulated the pole so that the noose opened into a wide loop and dropped over his quarry's head. It settled round the great black neck. The cord ran back along the pole to Hal's hand. He gave it a yank that snugged it about the animal's throat.

The bull, with a savage bellow, tried to pull his head down through the hatch, but the rope tightened and held him fast. Hal was not trusting to his own strength. He knew his strength was no match for the bull's. He had already looped his end of the rope round the fender and made it fast.

Now it was bull versus fender. Which would prove the stronger? The fender danced and buckled and groaned. If the fender went, Hal's seat which was strapped to it would go too. The seat bounced up and down like a yoyo, and Hal bounced with it.

The Powerwagon was coming. Hal waved it on. Mali speeded up, and the big cage in the back of the Land-Rover rattled and banged as the car crashed over stones and holes.

Roger stared wide-eyed at this most unusual sight, a bull-headed truck. The Greeks had told stories of a centaur, half man and half horse. What would they think of this monster with an animal head, metal body, and wheels?

He saw the desperate efforts the buffalo was making to back out of the trap in which he found himself. If the rope snapped, he would be lost.

'Step on it, Mali!' he urged.

He saw Hal waving to him, directing him to the other side of the Ford. In a flash he caught his brother's idea.

He called back to the men in the rear around the cage.

'Open the cage door!' Then to Mali, 'Swing round and back up.'

Now they were close enough to hear the thrashing and crashing as the big bull turned the fittings of the cab into mincemeat in his fight to get loose. A lot of repairs would be necessary. This was taking 'em alive the expensive way. It was hard on the car and it was also hard on the animal.

Mali turned out, then backed up until the open cage door was against the open door of the Ford.

'Slack away!' Roger shouted. Hal loosed the catching-rope from the fender. The bull, with the strain on his neck relieved, promptly drew down his head and began to back out of the car.

He could not see where he was going for a buffalo's eyes are planted at the front of his head, not on the sides.

Before he could realize what was happening to him, he had backed into the cage.

Mali pulled forward a few feet so that the cage door would have room to swing shut, and Hal, who had already left his seat and run round to the back of the Powerwagon, closed the heavy iron door.

The animal bellowed with rage and frustration, rushed from side to side, striking the iron bars with his bony helmet and making the heavy Powerwagon rock. He might break his horns on the bars, and certainly he would bruise his flesh even through that thick hide. He must be quieted or he would destroy both himself and his cage.

Hal got out the curare gun. He watched for his chance to pump a shot into this red-eyed, foaming bunch of fury.

Before he could do so, the bull's rage suddenly sim-
mered down. He stood with legs braced apart, dripping
with sweat, blood, and foam, head hanging. He was a
picture of weariness and despair. Then his legs buckled
beneath him and he collapsed on the steel floor.

15 | Baby-sitter to a bull

HEART attack, Hal thought. Even a bull buffalo cannot go on for ever. This bull had been one of the leaders in the attack upon the camp, and he had probably been well battered when he had collided head-on with the trucks. Then he had been chased until he was tired by an engine that never got tired, he had undergone the unusual experience of climbing into the driver's seat and pursuing a man through a hole in the roof, he had been noosed, he had fought for liberty, and then he had tested his strength against iron bars. Now he was broken in spirit as well as in body. And Hal knew that unless he acted promptly, he would have nothing but a dead animal for all his pains.

This was no job for a curare gun. The animal did not need quieting, but reviving.

Hal leaped back into the cab and got the coramine syringe.

Coramine is a heart stimulant used by catchers when an animal shows signs of dying from exhaustion, fear, or shock.

To inject the drug, the syringe must be placed against the hide. But the bull lay in the middle of the cage and Hal could not reach any part of him through the bars. There was no help for it – he must join the dangerous beast inside the cage.

He opened the cage door, stepped inside, and closed the door behind him. The bull snorted angrily and struggled

to his feet. Here was his enemy just where he wanted him.
He feared the thing in the man's hand. It had a sharp end
like a horn. But if he could get one of his own horns into
the man first and push it home, he would be rid of this
pest for good and all.

He threw his ton at Hal, but the acrobatic naturalist
was no longer there and the horns went harmlessly
through the bars. The bull drew back and charged again,
and again Hal side-stepped.

This time Hal was not so lucky. He found himself
pinned between the animal's right hip and the iron grating. If enough of the animal's weight was used against
him, he could be minced between those iron bars like flesh
in a meat-grinder.

He was smeared with the sweat of the overstrained
animal and blood from its bruises. The pressure on his
body was tremendous, but his arm was free and he had
the presence of mind to jab the syringe into the bull's
thigh and inject the stimulant. At the same instant the bull
fell to the floor, his last spark of energy gone.

It would take twenty minutes or half an hour for the
stimulant to act. Perhaps it had been given too late and
the bull was already dead.

'Better get out of there,' Roger called. 'He's apt to rear
up again any minute.'

'No,' Hal said. 'He's pooped. I just hope we won't lose
him altogether.'

Hal hovered over the beast like an anxious mother. He
placed his hand over the nostrils. He felt nothing and his
anxiety increased.

Then there was a pulse of warmth against his hand. It
was very weak, but it showed that breathing and heart
action had not stopped.

Hal looked over the hide for wounds and made a mental note of them. They must be treated later – *if* the animal lived.

It was a big 'if'. The sweat on the beast's flanks had chilled. The great eyes that had glared so savagely were closed. Hal's father would not think much of him if he lost his first buffalo.

He could imagine him saying, as he had so often said before, 'Remember, you're here to take animals alive, not dead.'

He felt a sort of tenderness towards this helpless, heart-sick beast. From creases in the skin he plucked out ticks that the egrets had overlooked. His placed his hand again over the nostrils, but though he held it there for a long time he felt nothing.

Roger was peering in through the bars.

'How does it feel to be a baby-sitter to a buffalo?' he laughed.

Hal was not amused.

'I only hope I'm not attending a funeral. What's the matter with that coramine? It should have acted by this time.'

Had the heart stopped? Hal was no fool as a naturalist, but he was still learning, and that was one thing he had forgotten to ask his father – how do you take a buffalo's pulse?

Another ten minutes of anxious waiting, and Hal again tested for breath. Was it just imagination, or did he feel a slight come-and-go of warm and cool? Yes, there was no doubt about it. His own heart leaped.

'He's coming through!' he shouted.

The bull came through fast. His breathing grew steadily stronger. His eyes opened and the first thing they lit upon was Hal. But in those eyes there was not the same hate as before.

Perhaps the buffalo, being a highly intelligent animal, understood that this man could have killed him but had not. Possibly he was not so bad after all. He could even be a friend. He felt Hal's fingers plucking out the painful ticks from his hide. And he could even look at the syringe with appreciation. He had been stabbed by it, and now he felt better.

He was just tired. Convinced that he did not need to fear this human, he closed his eyes and slept. Hal quietly left the cage.

'Take him to camp,' he told Mali. 'Go easy – don't shake him up any more than necessary. You'll have to give the Ford a tow. That bull dancing a jig in the cab didn't do it any more good than a bull in a china-shop.'

In half an hour the boys were after their second buffalo.

The Ford had been left in camp with a mechanic hard at work repairing or replacing the battered controls. The Powerwagon had also been left, rather than disturb the buffalo by removing the cage.

Hal had strapped his seat to the fender of a Chev catcher driven by Joro, while Mali and Roger followed in a Powerwagon bearing another cage.

The herd was grazing quietly about a mile from camp. Hal picked out a splendid bull which was wandering a little apart from the rest of the herd.

Joro drove the car alongside, and Hal neatly slipped the noose over the bull's head.

It had all been very easy up to this point. Now it began to be difficult. The bull did not take kindly to his new necklace. He tried to shake it off.

When this did not work, he went plunging away and might have broken the line if Hal had not let it out bit by bit, as a fisherman plays a fish.

Changing his tactics, the bull wheeled about, bellowed, then came on the run straight for the truck.

'Face him!' Hal shouted. 'Take him on the bumper.'

Joro didn't need to be told. He had had enough experience to know that when a buffalo, rhino or elephant charges, the car must be turned to face the charge. It cannot easily be overturned if struck in front. But if the beast manages to give it a blow on the side it may spin upside-down.

There was another good reason why Joro did not allow a flank attack. It would expose Hal to the greatest possible danger, for his small seat strapped to the fender was on the side towards the bull.

'Swing round!' Hal yelled, and accompanied the order with a swing of his hand.

Joro seemed to be trying, but there were many stones and hummocks in the way.

Then suddenly the engine went dead. Hal's heart sank. Whether the motor had stopped by accident or Joro had deliberately stalled it, Hal would never know.

But he did know that he stood a very good chance of being killed. He worked feverishly to unfasten the lifebelt that held him to his seat. The buckle was stubborn. He shouted again to Joro. Joro stepped on the starter, the engine roared, then stalled again. Joro waved his hands as if to say he could do nothing more.

A column of dust rose from the flying heels of the bull. The head was lowered, the tough forehead was ready for the crash. Joro was leaping out of the car now and placing himself at a safe distance. Hal at last pulled open the buckle and threw off the belt.

He scrambled up on to the hood just as the bull struck the very spot where he had been sitting. The chair was smashed into a pulp. The fender behind it was crushed. The heavy car toppled over on to its side. Hal slid off the hood and leaped clear.

He had not forgotten his job and was still hanging on to the catching-pole. Hot with anger, he turned upon Joro:

'Did you want to get me killed?'

'No, *bwana*,' Joro said, but the savage eyes seemed to say yes.

'I noticed you took good care to save yourself,' Hal said bitterly.

'All the men did,' Joro reminded him. 'Why not? It was the thing to do.'

It was so. The men in the back of the truck had jumped clear, and Hal had to admit it was the thing to do. Still, he suspected Joro.

The bull gave him no time to think about this. He was making one rush after another, trying to escape the pull of the rope. The men heaved the car back into an upright position. The Powerwagon carrying the cage had come up, and the men from both cars now undertook the dangerous job of catching and hobbling the frantic animal.

Hal had looped the end of the line round the car bumper, for a thirteen-stone man could not hold a one-ton bull.

Toto started the risky game. He dashed in and grabbed the buffalo by the tail. The bull turned sharply and tried to get at him.

But a buffalo is no cat. He cannot reach his tail. And he is no mule. He has not acquired the habit of kicking with his hind hooves. He will stamp upon his victim if he gets a chance, but kicking is not part of his act. So long as Toto could hang on, he was comparatively safe.

The bull, whirling to get at Toto, was not paying enough attention to the other men. They sneaked up on his flanks and tried to get nooses round his feet. When the bull chased them, they skipped just far enough away so that he was brought up short by the rope and could not reach them.

This worked well enough until the rope broke. It snapped close to the bumper, and the bull, trailing a hundred feet of line, went after the men in earnest.

Now there was nothing to stop him. Dragging Toto behind him, he chose to single out an African called Kenyono, who promptly made for a tree and scrambled up just one hot breath ahead of the bull.

He did not quite succeed in climbing clear. He hung from a branch and his dangling legs were within reach of the brute's teeth.

But the bull did not attack with his teeth. He had another weapon even more dangerous – his tongue. That tongue is as rough as a coarse file or wood-rasp. It will scrape off the bark of a tree or grind up thorns, twigs, sharp-edged elephant grass and tough stalks of papyrus.

The bull began licking the dangling legs. The skin came off like tissue-paper, and gobs of flesh down to the bone.

In a moment both legs were streaming with blood and the African was screaming for help.

Roger did some quick thinking. He had one of the foot-nooses in his hand. He slipped it over the bull's muzzle and pulled it tight. That made him close his mouth at once.

'Hope he bit his tongue,' Roger said.

Kenyono dropped from the tree and two men helped him to a truck. The other men continued their efforts to noose the animal's feet. Time and again they barely escaped being gored by the sweeping horns.

They got a noose over the front hooves and drew it tight.

The bull stumbled, fell on his right shoulder, and threw his hind feet in the air.

Toto, the tail-hanger, had been watching for this, and as the feet went up he grabbed a noose from the man next to him and flipped it in place.

Bound both fore and aft, the bull lay on his side, snorting and blowing like a porpoise.

The Powerwagon rolled up with Mali at the wheel. In the back of the truck was the buffalo-size cage. The Chev took its position in front of the Land-Rover, and a cable was played back through the cage and looped round the helpless animal just behind the shoulders and forelegs.

The Chev advanced, using all its four-wheel-drive power, the cable tightened, and the squirming animal was dragged up a greased ramp into the cage.

The prize was taken to camp, and the injured Kenyono received prompt medical treatment from the not too expert but willing hands of Hal Hunt.

16 | Roger takes a ride

'LET me snag the next one,' pleaded Roger.

Hal had noosed two buffalo. Roger considered that it was his turn.

Hal objected. His own narrow escape from being crushed between a bull's head and a steel fender chilled his blood whenever he thought of it.

'It's no game for kids,' he said.

Age thirteen looked up at age nineteen with fire in his eye.

'What's that you called me? Watch your language, you young squirt, or I'll take you over my knee and pound some sense into you.'

Hal looked at the broad shoulders and strong frame of his younger brother. The 'kid' was coming along fast. It wouldn't be many years now before the two of them would be evenly matched.

'Suppose I have no right to "kid" you,' he admitted. 'But – take a look at this chair.'

He ran his fingers over the splinters of wood and twists of metal that had once been a chair. The bits and pieces of it were plastered against the fender. No carpenter on earth could ever put it together again. Hal unstrapped it from the car and threw it away. He turned to Roger.

'Suppose you had been in that thing when the big boy arrived.'

'Do you think I'd stay in it until he got there?' Roger demanded. 'You got out, didn't you? Why couldn't I?' When his brother showed no sign of relenting, Roger added, 'Let's put it to Dad.'

They went in to their father's cot and repeated their argument. John Hunt was suffering considerable pain, but his look softened into a smile as he studied his boys.

'Hal doesn't want you to be hurt,' he said to Roger. 'I don't either. But you, Hal, must realize that this "kid", as you call him, is almost a man. We don't want to stop him from becoming one. He'll become one only if he takes his chance along with other men. Let him ride the chair.'

Roger gave a whoop that betrayed him as still being pretty much of a boy. He dashed out to the supply wagon, got another chair and lashed it to the fender of the Land-Rover that was to be used this time as the catching-vehicle. And he found himself a lasso, such as the cowboys used in the American West. He had practised with it for hours – now was his chance to see if he could use it to make a real capture.

But when Joro began to climb into the driver's seat of the Land-Rover, Hal checked him.

'You and I will go in the cage truck,' he said, 'just for a change. Mali, you drive the Land-Rover.'

Hal wanted Joro where he could watch him. He climbed in beside this doubtful fellow, who was perhaps a leopard-man and perhaps had tried to kill him only half an hour before. There were too many perhapses about Joro. But it was certain that he was a good driver and a good hunter, and he must be considered innocent until he was proved guilty.

The herd had moved into the shade to escape the growing heat of the day. Some were lying down, asleep, others slept standing up, others wallowed comfortably in a muddy marsh beside the river. All stayed close together for safety except the biggest bulls, who were so sure of their own strength that they thought they did not need the protection of the herd. They didn't want to be disturbed by the grunting of the cows and the screaming of the babies. They had strayed away, each one by himself.

Roger selected one with shoulders like a football hero's and a head as solid as the door of a safe. Surely, Roger thought, this giant must be king of the herd. He pointed him out to Mali.

The great beast moved away at a slow, dignified walk as the car approached. The walk changed to a run, and the run to a gallop.

Mali did not stop for rocks, logs, or holes. Roger bounced like a rubber doll. This was his first time in a fender chair. He had never dreamed the ride could be so rough. Not trusting his lifebelt, he hung on with one hand while he held the lasso ready in the other.

Now they were close enough. Roger whirled the lasso three times round his head and let it fly. The loop settled down round a thorn-bush, and a yank on the rope might well have pulled Roger apart if Mali had not promptly ground to a stop.

Mali and the men in the back of the Land-Rover were laughing. Laughter came, too, from the following Power-wagon. Roger blushed a rosy red. A great hunter he was! Aiming at a buffalo and snagging a thorn-bush!

One of the men jumped down and pulled the loop free from the bush. Roger pulled in and coiled the rope as Mali started the car.

The bull had stopped and was looking back with a big grin on his ugly face – or so it seemed to Roger. Then with snort and a toss of his head he took to his heels, and the chase was on again.

At every bump Roger rose several inches about his seat. Half the time he was like an astronaut, weightless, flying through space. When he did come down on the iron seat, he hit it with a painful whack. How could anyone expect a fellow to throw a lasso from this bouncing, pounding car, worse than any wild horse?

Now he was close. He would try, but he was sure he would fail. At least he would choose a spot where there were no thorn-bushes.

Seizing his chance, he snaked the nylon noose out towards the big black head.

He let out a whoop worthy of any cowboy when he saw the rope tighten round the king's neck.

The line, made fast to the fender, brought the bull up short. The men spilled out of the cars to complete the capture. Even the two drivers, Mali and Joro, joined in the struggle, for this was a real giant and would not easily be hobbled.

The bull had turned to face his tormentors and stood still like something carved out of stone, except that his blazing eyes rolled from side to side, taking in every move.

He wouldn't be half so smart if we could blindfold him, thought Roger. He loosed himself from his chair, snatched a red blanket out of the car, and made for the animal's head.

Before he could get there, the beast let out a roar of defiance, leaped straight up into the air like a black balloon, pulled the line taut and snapped it as if it had been a silk thread. Then he struck out after the nearest African, who happened to be Joro.

The men stood with their mouths agape. They could not hope to keep up with that whirlwind. Joro's oiled, black body flashed in the sun as he ran for his life.

The man and bull passed close to Roger. The boy leaped for the trailing line, grabbed it, and held on. He could not even slow down the steam-engine. He was dragged head first over humps and hollows, sticks and stones, and through elephant grass whose razor edges sliced into his face and hands.

He couldn't care less. This was his bull and it was not going to escape him.

His toboggan ride was made a little easier by the blanket which got tangled round his shoulders and took some of the jolts.

The wild race came to a sudden halt. Roger, feeling considerably battered, raised himself on his elbow and looked. He brushed away the blood that seeped into his eyes from scratches on his forehead. What he saw made him leap to his feet and run to the assistance of the black hunter.

The bull had caught up with Joro and knocked him flat. Now he slid his right horn under the man and tossed him ten feet in the air as lightly as if he had been a bag of meal. Joro came down on a ridge of rock with a force that would have broken the back of an ordinary man.

He tried to rise, but got up only on his hands and knees before the buffalo's head went beneath him and tossed him again, making the black body spin in the air, then caught it as it came down and gave it still another skyward fling.

When the limp body sprawled to the ground, the angry buffalo stood up on his hind feet and brought his forefeet smashing down upon his victim. Joro tried to roll out of the way, but the hammer-like hooves found him again.

It was the buffalo's favourite method of attack. He would not be satisfied until he had separated bone from bone and crushed out every sign of life.

Seeing this ferocious beast at work, Roger heard a small voice telling him that he ought to be running the other way. But he ran on straight into trouble.

His brain, too, was racing. What could he do? He was no match for this huge bull. As for his blanket, he could never hope to get it over the bull's head and hold it there without any men to help him. He was sure the men were coming, but Joro would die before they arrived.

Then a crazy idea came into his head. It might work. If this bull was anything like his distant cousins in the bull-rings of Spain, he would go for a waving blanket.

Facing the bull, he gripped the blanket by two corners and let it billow out on the breeze.

The bull stopped his deadly trampling. He glared at the red, flapping thing. Then with a snort of rage he charged.

When he got to where the red thing had been it was no longer there. The young toreador had flipped it into the air so that the bull passed beneath it.

The bull wheeled about. There it was again, the great red thing daring him to come on. Roger was feeling the flush of victory. If he could just keep on bamboozling this silly beast until the men go there . . .

The bull charged. This time the wind played pranks with the blanket. It did not soar up out of the way as it was supposed to do.

The bull caught it on his horns, wrenched it out of Roger's hands, tossed it on the ground and proceeded to trample it just as he had trampled Joro. When it lay still he sniffed at it, decided it was dead, and turned his atten-

tion to Joro, who was dismally trying to get up on his
feet.

Would the men never come? Roger did not realize that
what had seemed to him many minutes had only been a
matter of seconds. Now he heard the men coming, but he
could not wait for them. The bull was advancing upon
Joro. The man would certainly be killed if he got another
beating from those sledge-hammer hooves.

Roger jumped in front of the bull, waved his arms and
shouted, hoping to scare him off. He might as well have
tried to scare the Rock of Gibraltar.

The bull came on, horns lowered. Roger instinctively
seized the horns. If he could just manage to hang on, those
horns couldn't hurt him.

The bull angrily tossed his head. Up went Roger like a
rocket. The first of the men came bursting through the
bushes in time to see Roger in the air. His hands had been
jerked loose from the horns. He came down with an un-
graceful sprawl on the beast's back.

The men came pouring in, shouting, grabbing at the
bull's tail, legs, horns.

This was too much, even for a king. He shook off his
pursuers and took to his heels.

Roger had a free ride. He found himself half straddling
the beast, gripping an ear with one hand and a horn with
the other. If he slid off, this killer would take great pleasure in smashing him to smithereens with those meat-
chopping hooves.

But the buffalo knew from long experience how to get
rid of an undesired visitor. The lion attacks a four-footed
animal by leaping upon its back. The leopard does the
same. A clever buffalo, when thus attacked, looks for a
tree with a low branch. He rushes through beneath it,

hoping the branch will scrape his enemy from his back.

The bull headed for a low-slung mopani tree. Roger did not wake up to his danger until it was almost too late.

He had to make a lightning-quick decision between staying on board until he was brushed off or perhaps squeezed to death by a low branch, and slipping off to run the risk of being danced upon by a ton of angry bull.

He let go and landed hard on a pile of rocks.

The bull had wonderful brakes. He stopped his mad run within his own length, spun about, and prepared to mash his enemy into the rocks. His snorting nose was within a foot of Roger's face.

Roger seized the only weapon at hand. He grabbed a heavy rock and swung it with all his strength against that great twitching nose.

He did this by instinct – without a notion that he was doing exactly the right thing. The tip of the nose is the one tender spot of the buffalo's anatomy. A good hard smash on that one vital spot takes all the fight out of him.

The bull drew back, his head swaying, his eyes popping with surprise.

Before he could collect his scattered wits, the men were upon him. Some held him by the broken lasso, some gripped him by the horns. As he leaped and bucked, others watched their chance and finally noosed the flying heels together, then the forefeet. The bull fell over on his right side, still puffing and snorting defiance.

The cars were brought in with some difficulty because of the thick underbrush and rocks. The first thing to do was to lay the injured Joro on the floor in the back of the Land-Rover, using as a bed the red blanket of Toreador Roger Hunt.

The captured bull was hauled up into his cage. Toto slipped in, cut the foot-nooses, slid out again and slammed shut the door before the bewildered animal could get to his feet.

Back in camp, Joro was bedded down in his tent, and Hal gave him a shot of a quarter-grain of morphine to relieve his pain. The drug acted within a few minutes. Hal went over the African's body for breaks and bruises. There were bruises aplenty, but no breaks. To the men who had crowded into the tent, Hal reported:

'His bones must be made of rubber to stand all that. He'll be all right.'

Joro was grinning from ear to ear. That was not like Joro. He was usually grim and sour.

'What's so funny?' Hal asked.

'The young *bwana*,' Joro said, looking at Roger. Then he went on to tell about the boy's exploits – the toboggan ride at the end of the lasso, his performance with the fluttering red blanket, the way he had jumped in between the bull and Joro and grabbed the animal's horns. The men roared with laughter as Joro described the boy's rocket flight, how he had come down smack on the animal's back, his wild ride until he had let go and landed on the rock pile, and then – that smash on the nose!

The African has his own sense of humour. It is tickled by stories of accidents. He thinks it very funny if someone takes a tumble – even if the one who tumbles is himself.

Roger slipped out of the tent before Joro finished. He still heard the men laughing as if they would burst their sides. He didn't like being laughed at.

Before the day was over, he found they were not laughing at him but with him. When any of them passed him, they bowed with new respect and gave him a warm smile.

They were proud of him. Hal was proud of him. His father was proud of him.

He couldn't understand this, for he had only done what he had to do from one moment to the next. In a way, it had been fun. Now that he thought about it, it was even funny, and he could laugh about it too.

17 | The bag of poison

HAL had not forgotten his promise to visit the sick chief.

It was night before he could go. Then he slipped out of the camp and walked up the hill.

The people of the village had already turned in. The doors of the mud huts were shut. The light of a flickering fire inside came from some of the small windows. Other windows were completely dark – the family slept.

Hal moved quietly. There was no reason to disturb anyone – in fact he would rather not. Especially he didn't want to meet the witch-doctor.

He knew the man hated him intensely. That was natural. The witch-doctor had failed to cure the chief. If Hal succeeded, the people would lose faith in their witch-doctor.

It would be better for the witch-doctor if the chief died. Then he could say:

'I told you so. I told you the white man's bad magic would kill him. You should have listened to me.'

Hal stopped at the chief's door. He listened for voices inside but heard nothing. He pressed open the door, slid inside, and closed the door behind him.

The place was dimly lighted by the wavering flame of a home-made, hippo-fat candle. Most of the room was in darkness. The candle lit the face of the chief, who was sound asleep.

Just what he needs, Hal thought. I won't disturb him.

He would stay awhile – possibly the chief would wake. Hal retreated into a dark corner and sat down on the mat.

He listened to his patient's breathing. It was regular and normal. There was no flush on the face, no sweat, no fever, no tossing about. The drugs administered by 'Doctor' Hal Hunt had done their good work.

Hal got to thinking about the events of the day. After a long time he found himself getting drowsy. He roused himself and looked at his watch. He had been there an hour. No use waiting longer – the chief might sleep until morning.

Hal was about to rise when he heard a slight sound outside the hut. He listened intently, but there was nothing more. He must have been mistaken. No, there it was again – a slight brushing sound as of a bare foot on the sand.

Then, slowly and silently, the door opened. Someone was edging in, being very careful to make no noise. Perhaps it was one of the chief's wives with some food. Hal was about to speak, but on second thoughts held his tongue.

The door was closed again as quietly as it had been opened. The figure slowly approached the sleeping chief. As it came out of the dark into the candlelight, Hal recognized the witch-doctor.

Again he was about to speak and again he held his tongue. What was this fellow up to? In his left hand he held a small leather bag, and in his right something sharp.

He stopped and listened. He looked warily around the room.

Then he kneeled on the mat beside the chief. Now Hal could plainly see his face. Why, Hal wondered, does the face of a cruel man look so much worse than the face of a cruel animal?

Still, it was possible the man meant no harm. Perhaps he had come to wake the chief and speak with him or give him some medicine.

The witch-doctor carefully studied the sleeping man. Then, before Hal could realize what was going on, he lightly touched the sharp thing against the chief's arm.

The chief did not wake. Hal guessed that the sharp thing was a *chook*. That is a quill of the brush-tailed porcupine, so sharp that it can go through the skin without being felt. It takes the place of the white man's hypodermic needle.

But why make this tiny puncture in the chief's skin? What good, or harm, would that do?

The wizard laid down his *chook* and opened the leather bag. He inserted the tip of his finger and it came out covered with a dark paste. He was about to rub the paste into the hole made by the chook when Hal let loose.

'What the devil are you up to?' he shouted.

The words were in English but the shout was enough to do two things – wake the patient and freeze the witch-doctor as if he had been suddenly turned to stone.

The chief at once took in the picture – the *chook* on the mat, the leather bag, the dark smear on the finger-tip, Hal running in out of the shadows.

The witch-doctor leaped to his feet and made for the door. Hal grappled with him, threw him down, and sat on him. Men and women came running.

All they could understand at first was that their precious witch-doctor was being sat upon by that meddling stranger. They pulled Hal away and the witch-doctor got to his feet, spluttering with injured dignity. Again he started for the door.

'Don't let him go,' the chief called. 'Bring him here.'

Men blocked the door. They hesitated to lay hands on the wizard. Some of the more courageous seized him and brought him to the chief's side.

'Release my friend,' commanded the chief. Hal, suddenly free, came to stand beside the witch-doctor.

A hush fell over the crowd. It was like a court with a judge about to pronounce sentence.

'The man you hold,' the chief said quietly, 'was about to end my life. You see this *chook*. As I slept, he used it upon me. You see its mark on my arm. Force him to show the middle finger of his right hand. You see that dark stain. Search among his claws and feathers and you will find the bag from which it came.'

The bag was found. One of the elders opened it. He picked up a small stick and dipped the end of it into the bag. It came out covered with a black, sticky paste like tar. It was the same as the stuff on the witch-doctor's finger-tip, the stuff he had been about to rub into the cut on the chief's arm.

'You all know what this is,' said the chief.

'Except me,' Hal said. 'Is it a poison?'

'It is.'

'I guessed that it might be – that's why I stopped him.'

'You did well,' the chief said. 'If you had not, my people would now be making ready to bury me.'

'It acts so fast?'

'It kills in a few minutes. We use it on our arrowheads. It is made from the sap of the mrichu tree.'

Hal, as a student of animals and plants, knew the tree.

'I have often seen it,' he said. 'We call it the acocanthera. The ground under it is covered with bees and beetles and humming-birds – all dead.'

'Yes. They drink from the purple flowers of the mrichu and they die of the poison.'

'How do you make this paste for the arrows?'

'We boil the bark for many hours. So we get a thick, black syrup. We add to it the venom of snakes, the poison of spiders, and the roots of deadly weeds. A live shrew is thrown in and we boil it all again.'

'How can you tell when it is strong enough to kill?'

'We make a small cut in a man's arm near the shoulder and let the blood trickle down the arm. We touch the lower end of this trickle with a little bit of the poison. Its touch makes the blood turn black. The blackness goes up the trickle of blood towards the cut. We wipe it away just before it reaches the cut. If the black climbs slowly or stops, we know the poison is too weak. If it climbs fast we know it is strong.'

The witch-doctor broke out into a torrent of argument.

When he had finished, the chief said to Hal:

'He says this is not poison, but only good medicine. Very well, we will test it.'

He gave an order to the elder who had opened the bag. The elder took up the *chook*. In spite of the witch-doctor's angry protests, the elder made a slight incision in the medicine man's upper arm, just enough to draw the blood.

A tiny stream of blood ran down the witch-doctor's arm to the elbow.

The old man touched the blood at the elbow with the end of the paste-smeared stick.

The blood at once turned black. The blackness climbed the arm with amazing speed towards the cut.

The witch-doctor was wrenching and twisting now, trying to get away from the men who held him and crying like a terrified child. The chief spoke to him firmly.

'I am telling him,' the chief said to Hal, 'that he will be a dead man in three minutes unless he makes a full confession. He must admit that he was trying to poison me, and he must say why.'

The blackness had now gone up like a snake half-way to the cut.

The witch-doctor, pale-faced, eyes popping with terror, broke out into a rapid babble. Up went the black snake. Just before it reached the opening through which it would have gone its killing way into the bloodstream, the chief gave a sharp order. The elder wiped the witch-doctor's arm clean.

'We have saved his life,' the chief said, 'though he does not deserve it. He has made full confession. He was jealous of your power to heal. With all his magic he could not cure me, and then you cured me with a few small white things. The people were laughing at him. He wanted me to

die so that he could say your medicine had killed me. For
this evil he should be burned. But we of this village are
not cruel. He shall live, but he must leave the village and
trouble us never again.'

The sentence was carried out at once. The would-be
murderer was allowed to collect a few of his personal be-
longings and was sent out into the night. Hal returned to
camp.

He did not sleep well, for he had an uneasy feeling that
this was not quite the end of the story. If he understood
the evil gleam he had last seen in the witch-doctor's eyes,
the Hunt family and Hal in particular could expect more
trouble, soon.

18 | Killers' pledge

THE night was dark, and the witch-doctor's journey through country where a lion, elephant or buffalo might be lurking behind any bush was not too pleasant.

At every step his bitterness and his passion for revenge grew. He would show that white magician and his brother and father that it was dangerous to get in the way of a clever witch-doctor.

He was not aimlessly wandering about. He knew exactly where he was going and what he was going to do. After some five miles of winding trail he saw lights shining between the tree-trunks of a patch of woodland.

He stopped at the edge of the woods. The sound of voices told him that many men were gathered in conference beneath the trees.

He knew who these men were. He was one of them. But no one may walk into a meeting of the Leopard Society unannounced. If he should try it, he would get a poisoned arrow in his chest before he could come out of the shadows.

The witch-doctor made the peculiar cry of the leopard. It was a good imitation. The leopard has a number of ways of expressing himself. He can growl, and he can roar, and he can scream. But usually he saws wood, just as the witch-doctor did now.

It sounded quite like a coarse saw going through a log.

After each 'saw' the breath was noisily drawn in. So every time there was a double sound. It was something like 'Saw-ah! Saw-ah! Saw-ah! Saw-ah!'

Immediately the talking stopped. Then someone came swinging a lantern. He held the light up to the witch-doctor's face.

'Ah, it is you, great one. We are honoured that you have come.'

He led the way back to the lighted circle. The witch-doctor took his place on slightly higher ground with the leaders. A leopard costume was brought to him and he put it on.

Here was a strange sight – twenty men all clothed in leopard skins, masks over their heads, curved iron spikes like leopards' claws projecting from their fingers, leopard pads strapped to their feet so that wherever they went they would leave the track of a leopard.

It seemed like a fevered dream. But the Leopard Society is no figment of the imagination. It is to be found throughout Central and West Africa. The police have forced it back into the hills, but there it still exists. Different branches of it go under different names, the Idiong Society, the Ekpe Leopards, and so on. Within three years, in one small area of West Africa, 196 men, women, and children were murdered by the leopard-men.

Why? The reasons vary from place to place. Sometimes the purpose is to punish a village that has become too rich and powerful. Sometimes the killing is prompted by hate of the white man. Often the human leopards kill other humans just to get the heart, the eyeballs, the tongue, the ears or some other members which are supposed to have magic powers as medicine or charms.   Make no mistake about it – most Africans are kind and good. Every year more of them go to school. Every year some of the old superstitions die. But there is a long way yet to go. Think of it – when the Congo became independent of Belgium, this great African nation, eighty-eight times as big as Belgium itself, had only sixteen university graduates.

There are still millions of Africans who have never spent one day in school. Without education, they still believe strange things – that a leopard-man can turn into a leopard, that the heart of a strong man will make you strong if you eat it, and that no white man can be trusted.

One of the leaders spoke.

'Chief among us is the friend who has just come. Let him speak that we may obey.'

The witch-doctor rose. Here was a man whom even the leopard-men feared, for he could work dark and dangerous magic. They listened to him in respectful silence.

'There is one among you,' he began, 'who has not kept his pledge. He solemnly promised to kill and has not killed. His name is Joro. I call upon him to stand.'

Joro slowly got to his feet. Dressed as a leopard-man, he looked quite different from the Joro of the Hunt camp. Besides the leopard skin on his back and the steel slaws on his hands, his chest was spotted with strange colours and his face painted to make him look more like the savage beast he was supposed to represent. But now he hung his head like a guilty schoolboy.

'A week ago,' the witch-doctor said, 'You, Joro performed a sacred ritual and made a pledge. What was that pledge?'

Joro looked helplessly about him. 'I pledged,' he said in a low voice, 'I pledged to kill three men of my safari.'

'And who were they?'

'A father and two sons. Their name is Hunt.'

'And have you fulfilled your promise?'

'I tried. The three were with me in a canoe. There was a hippopotamus in the river and many crocodiles. The hippo attacked, and I held the canoe so that he would strike it, and the canoe was smashed, and I left the three at the mercy of the crocodiles. The father was nearly killed but the others saved him. Even now the father lies helpless between life and death. I could do no more.'

'And was that all?'

'No. I tried again. The elder son was in the catching-chair. A bull buffalo charged. I held the car in its place so that the buffalo would crush the man. The buffalo destroyed the chair – but the man was not in it. He escaped. He was too quick for me.'

'Two failures,' the witch-doctor said grimly. 'Anything else?'

'The younger son. I planned that a buffalo should kill him.'

Joro hesitated.

'Go on,' demanded the witch-doctor. 'Did you carry out your plan?'

'Instead, it was I who was nearly killed. It was the boy who prevented my death. If it had not been for him, I would not be standing before you now. He was very brave. He is but a boy, but he is a man. All three are good men. I cannot kill them. I beg you to relieve me from this pledge.'

'That cannot be done,' said the witch-doctor fiercely. 'If you do not carry out your pledge you must die.'

The threat did not seem to frighten Joro. He lifted his head and looked back at the witch-doctor with an air of defiance.

'Do with me as you will,' he said. 'Better one death than three.'

'It will not be one death,' replied the witch-doctor. 'You have a wife and four children. If you do not fulfil your oath, all six of you will pay with your lives.'

Joro's head sank again on his chest. He was a picture of sorrow and defeat. His companions watched him and waited. They were so still that they seemed scarcely to be breathing. The witch-doctor was also content to wait, a savage glint of victory in his eye. He knew he had won.

At last Joro spoke, but without lifting his head. His voice was low and very sad.

'I will try again,' he said.

19 | Tallest animal on earth

'GIRAFFES!'

Mali broke into the Hunt tent to make the announcement as it was just beginning to get light. Hal and Roger, with a hard day behind them, would have liked to sleep longer. But this was exciting news.

'Where?' Hal asked sleepily.

'Just outside the camp. Five of them.'

John Hunt spoke. 'Wish I could help you, boys. Nailing down a giraffe is a real job. Try to get two if you can – a male and a female. The Rio Zoo wants a pair.'

'Will they pay enough to make it worth while for me to get up?' grumbled Roger.

'Would you get up for six thousand pounds?'

Roger's eyes opened wide. He and his brother leaped out of bed and pulled on their clothes in such a hurry that Roger got his trousers on hind side before and Hal broke a bootlace.

One would have thought they were money mad. They were not – usually. But this kind of money was hardly to be made every day. In two minutes they were out of the tent.

There they were, only a few hundred yards from the camp, five handsome giraffes. Four were full grown, one was a baby. But what a baby! A giraffe on the day it is born is six feet tall.

They were all looking at the camp with the greatest curiosity. It is said that curiosity killed a cat. If curiosity kills, then all giraffes would have been dead long ago. There is no animal on earth more curious about things, more anxious to see what is going on.

Hal remembered the native story about the giraffe's curiosity. In the beginning, God gave them normal necks but long legs. Their long legs raised them so high that they couldn't see beneath the trees. So they tried to see over the tops of the trees. They stretched and stretched and stretched their necks, and the higher they stretched the better the view, and so they stretched some more. And now they stand twenty feet high and can look over the usual flat-topped acacia tree. And if they keep on getting taller some day they will be able to look straight into heaven, so say the tellers of tales.

In the early morning sun the golden hides looked very rich with their dark-brown spots.

'What I want to know,' Roger put in, 'is how he ever pumps blood up that skyscraper neck.'

'Just by having a big pump. His heart is forty times as big as yours. It weighs twenty-five pounds. He has the world's highest blood-pressure. The jugular vein in his neck is nearly two inches across, and blood shoots up it like water through a fire-hose.'

'But when he puts his head down to the ground, what then? All that pressure would blow his head off.'

'No. He has a fancy set of valves that slow down the blood. Don't worry. Nature has done a good job on him.'

A snort behind them made them look round. There was Colonel Bigg with his gun.

'What do you kids know about the giraffe?' he said

sarcastically. 'I'll tell you about the giraffe. He's the silliest thing on earth. Look at those long, skinny legs – what good are they? One crack with a cricket bat and they'd break like pipe stems. And that neck – you could tie a knot in it. Giraffes eat nothing but leaves. They can't even growl. They're not dangerous. Tell you what I'll do.' Colonel Bigg was feeling bigger every minute. His efforts so far to prove himself a great hunter had failed. Now he had his chance – he was sure he was more than a match for this flimsy, absurd imitation of an animal. He had heard that the giraffe is as timid as a mouse. 'If you're going to hunt 'em, I'm going with you. I'll show you how easy it is to tackle one of those walking telegraph poles.'

'If it's so easy,' Hal said, 'you won't need your gun. I'll take it.'

Reluctantly, Bigg parted with the gun. He set his hat at a jaunty angle. He was very proud of that hat. It made him look like an honest-to-goodness professional hunter.

'Who wants a gun?' he growled. 'All I need is my bare hands and a bit of rope. Come on, lads, I'll show you how it's done in a real safari.'

The boys and Bigg, with plenty of black helpers, climbed into a Land-Rover and a Bedford lorry. The lorry was a big four-ton job and carried a cage especially intended for the tallest of all living animals. The sides of the cage were fifteen feet high, but there was no roof – the last five feet of the bean-pole beast could project upwards into space.

'Run in on them fast,' Bigg told Mali, who was driving. But Roger ventured to correct him.

'No. Go easy. Don't scare them.'

Mali could choose between these two contrary orders.

He evidently thought Roger's idea more sensible, for he made the Land-Rover crawl as quietly as possible towards the inquisitive beasts. When he got within fifty feet of them and they began to show signs of nervousness, he stopped.

Now Roger could study them closely. Perhaps Bigg was right – they certainly looked very gentle and harmless. Their great brown eyes were as beautiful and tender as a girl's. Their eyelashes were long and lovely and a glossy jet black.

'Look as if they used mascara,' Roger said.

They were the Baringo type, the so-called five-horned giraffe. And there were the five horns – but they certainly didn't look dangerous. They were just stubby nubbins a few inches long and covered with hair. Roger asked Mali about the horns.

'Just decoration,' Mali said. 'He doesn't use them for fighting.'

'He's not a fighting animal.' Bigg put in.

Mali smiled. 'You'd be surprised. He uses his head – and not just for thinking. He strikes his enemy with the side of his head, not with his horns. And because his neck is so long he can give that head of his a terrific swing. I've seen one kill a leopard with a single swat.'

'A tall story,' Bigg said scornfully. 'They wouldn't hurt a fly. See that one with his mouth open. Why, he has no upper front teeth.'

'That's right.' Mali admitted. 'But he has plenty of big grinders back where you can't see them. Look at that one feeding on the thorn-tree. He has to have good teeth to grind up those thorns.'

'And a tough tongue.' Roger said, amazed to see a tongue a foot and a half long flick out and draw in the four-inch thorns where they could be crushed by the molars. Here again the giraffe was unusual. The whale had a longer tongue; but no land animal except the giant ant-eater could beat the giraffe.

'Another thing about these silly animals,' Bigg said with an air of superior knowledge. 'They can't make a sound.'

'I beg your pardon,' Mali objected. 'A lot of people think that – but it isn't so. The giraffe can make a moo or a grunt.'

Bigg snorted. 'A fine thing, that! An animal twenty feet tall and all he can do is moo or grunt! Even a jackal can make more noise than that.'

Mali turned and looked at Bigg gravely. 'Perhaps the giraffe doesn't need to make much noise. Animals are like people. Sometimes it's the people who talk the most who do the least.'

Bigg glared at him. 'I'll ask you to keep a civil tongue in your head. Remember who you are, you black scum. And if you think I talk too much and don't do anything, I'll show you.'

He opened the door and slid out into the catcher's seat. Roger was disappointed. He had hoped to do the catching himself.

'Let's go,' cried the colonel.

'Strap yourself in,' Mali suggested.

'Don't need to. We won't bump much. These creatures are as slow as molasses. Step on it. Go after that big one.'

Mali stepped on it. The bull giraffe cocked his head to one side and studied the car with his great brown eyes. Then he turned slowly and began lumbering away.

It was a very awkward lumber. The front feet went forward together, then the back feet came forward together outside the front feet. It was a sleepy, slow-motion kind of gait. The creature moved like a lazy rocking-chair. Bigg laughed.

'Clumsy fool! We'll catch him in no time.'

Roger watched the speedometer. It touched ten, then climbed to twenty, went up to thirty, and the giraffe was still rocking along well ahead of the car. The colonel was bouncing like popcorn. Now he tried to strap himself in, but could not.

'Hey!' he cried, 'Let up.'

But Roger nudged Mali, and Mali, with a grin, stepped a little harder. The speedometer showed forty miles an hour.

Now they were alongside the giraffe. He showed no signs of tiring. Every movement took him a good twenty feet. Bigg tried to unlimber his lariat, but he had to hold himself to his seat with both hands.

Suddenly a wall of heavy underbrush blocked the giraffe's path. He found himself trapped. He tried to cross in front of the car to more open country on the other side. He didn't quite make it. There was nothing for it but to leap over the car, and this he tried to do.

Bigg screamed with terror when he saw the great golden brown body soaring over him. He would never have believed a giraffe could look so enormous. He cringed in his chair, expecting to be mashed to a pulp.

The flying giraffe, more than twice as tall as the car, easily rose above it. But his leap was not quite long enough, and one foot came down on the roof.

It was a stout steel roof, and Bigg would never have thought it possible that one of those skinny, weak-looking legs could go through it. But what he had never realized was that this creature which looked so thin and frail actually weighed up to two tons.

When a foot with two tons of push behind it struck the roof, it went through like a knife through butter.

The colonel had left his precious hat on the seat beside Roger. The great hoof, a foot wide, was just the right size for that hat. It came down upon it squarely and turned it instantly into a brown pancake.

The foot had no sooner come down than it went up again, getting a few scratches from the torn metal, and the giraffe came to earth on the far side of the car and floated away.

Mali turned the car to follow him. The speed was forty and the ground was rougher than ever. Roger looked out and could see no colonel. He had bounced off.

Mali stopped the car and backed up. Bigg got unsteadily to his feet. He did not try to get back into the catcher's chair.

'Come, boy,' he managed to say, 'don't expect me to do all the work. It's your turn.'

Roger gleefully got out into the catcher's chair and firmly strapped himself in. Bigg climbed into the cab and surveyed his pancaked hat with amazement.

If he had stopped to think it out, he would not have been so surprised. After all, this two-ton weight on his hat was equal to that of twenty-five men each weighing twelve stone. And twenty five men sitting on a hat would not be too good for the hat.

With many a leap and bounce the speeding car pursued the smoothly gliding giraffe.

But suddenly the big fellow veered off to avoid something that had been concealed in the long grass. That something turned out to be a pride of five lions. (A group of lions is called a pride – why, don't ask me.)

The lions took off after the giraffe. Lions as well as

humans find giraffe meat very tasty.

The lion is the one dangerous enemy of the giraffe. A single lion doesn't dare attack – but a whole pride of lions rushing in at once may sometimes turn a giraffe into a good dinner.

The big bull giraffe was tiring. The lions streaking through the grass came up around him.

'Now you'll see,' Bigg declared. 'They'll turn him into mincemeat in ten seconds.'

One lion leaped for the giraffe's back, but it was too high a jump and he fell back sprawling on his rear end. Another leaped for the throat. The giraffe swung his sledge-hammer head and caught the air-borne lion in the stomach and sent him flying with all the wind and half the will knocked out of him.

Two attacked the front legs. Up went the great twelve-inch hooves and came down with a savage chopping effect that evidently caused severe internal injuries, for both the marauders slunk off, feeling very sick.

But it was the hind hooves of this magnificent, mild-mannered fighter that really took the cake. They flew out with such a powerful two-ton thrust that one lion died at once of a dislocated neck and another was knocked head over heels and lay on his back waving his feet in the air.

The Land-Rover rolled up, and the big cats that were still able to move crawled away. The giraffe was still watching them warily. That gave Roger his chance. He flung the lasso and the noose settled over the bull giraffe's neck.

The big bull began to lay about him furiously, and Hal, who had come up in the Bedford, feared for his brother's safety. He came running with the curare gun and fired the drug into the animal's thigh.

The medicine was given time to have its quieting effect. Then, without too much difficulty, the animal was led up into the cage, the cage door was closed, and the car driven back to camp – very slowly so that the hide of the magnificent beast should not be bruised by the iron bars.

The conquest of the female giraffe, the one with the six-foot baby, was more easily accomplished. The baby presented no problem at all. When he saw his mother in the cage, he promptly followed.

So the boys had a good report to make to their father. They not only had the big male and female, but a baby as a bonus.

'But I suppose it's not worth much,' Roger remarked.

'Don't you believe it,' said his father. 'It will bring just as much as a grown-up, perhaps more. I think Rio will be very happy to get the little fellow along with the others. Giraffes are enormously strong, as you found out, but their nerves are very delicate. The adults are apt to be much worried on this long trip to Rio and might even get sick, but the little fellow won't mind a thing so long as he is with his mother. He's really the best bet of the three. By the way, while you were gone Toto bagged a python. You'll see it in the snake cage. It's a beauty and ought to be worth almost as much as a giraffe, if only we can get it to a zoo alive. We have enough animals now for a shipment. The cargo ship *Kangaroo* will be arriving in Mombasa at the end of this week. I think that tomorrow morning we should start our animals to the coast, so that they'll get there in time to be put aboard that ship.'

20 | The deadly whiskers

THE boys found the python getting his dinner.

The great snake was nineteen feet long and as big round as Roger. It was as colourful as a rainbow, as graceful as a girl, and as mad as a hornet.

Ten men were with it inside the cage. One held its head, one its neck, and others gripped its body all the way down to the tip of its tail. They tried desperately to keep it straight, and it tried just as hard to whip loose, wrap its body round one of these pestiferous humans, and squeeze the life out of him.

Facing the big snake was Toto, who was trying to force large chunks of meat down the creature's throat, using a broom-handle as a poker. A newly captured python is too nervous to eat. He must be force-fed, otherwise he may starve to death.

Toto was performing a dangerous job. True, the python is not poisonous. He does not sting. But he can bite, and his savage teeth slant inwards, so that when they once get locked on your hand or your foot they hang on grimly until the snake is killed.

Therefore Toto, when he slipped a chunk of meat into the mouth, had to be very careful not to get his hand caught between those vicious jaws. Then he poked the meat back into the throat with the broom-handle. Gradually he pushed it farther back through the gullet, while the angry, wriggling snake tried to spit it out.

To prevent it from being thrown out, a rope was tied round the throat just in front of the bulge of meat. Then black hands massaged the food back until it reached the snake's belly. Another tourniquet was tied just in front of the stomach to prevent the food from shooting out like a ball from a cannon.

The same ticklish business had to be repeated with each chunk of meat. The first tourniquet was opened to let it pass, then closed, the food was stroked down the body, the second tourniquet opened to let it move into the stomach, then the tourniquet was once more pulled tight.

And all the time the men were pushed from one side to the other by the squirming body until it looked as if they were performing some strange, barbaric dance.

When the feeding was completed, the neck tourniquet was removed, but the stomach tourniquet was kept on for another ten minutes, until the powerful gastric juices had begun their work upon the meat and it was no longer likely that the food would be thrown out by the excited snake.

Pythons love water – so the cage was equipped with a large water-trough, and as soon as the men had gone the python slid into it.

There he lay quiet at last, enjoying the cool bath, only his head above water.

The boys went on to inspect the giraffes. They too were having a meal. Their dinner tables were fifteen feet high!

They were not exactly tables but boxes, strapped inside the cage near the top and full of acacia leaves.

Why so high? Giraffes are used to feeding from the top of thorn-trees. They spend much of the day feeding. If they had to bend their necks down all this time to eat, the strain would be too great and they might sicken and die.

The hippo was happy, at least as happy as a hippo can be without a river to wallow in. Palm leaves had been placed over the top of the cage to protect him from the sun. Tick birds had wriggled through the bars into the cage and were busily digging their dinner out of cracks in the hide.

Then there were the three buffalo cages. Two of the

buffalo were as savage as ever, but the one Hal had cared for greeted him with friendly grunts.

The hyenas paced back and forth in their cage with heads down as if deep in thought.

The baby leopards, Chu and Cha, needed no cage and tumbled about the camp head over heels in wild games with the dog, Zulu, and little Bab, the baby baboon.

Mother Bab sat and watched. When her baby played too roughly, or when he got into mischief among the cook's pans and dishes, she walked in and swatted him and said to him in very plain baboon language:

'Mind your manners.'

Every day the three hundred baboons of her tribe came to the edge of the camp. They seemed to argue with her.

'Why don't you come back with us to the trees and the river?'

But she politely refused. She would stay with the friends who had saved her young one's life. The other baboons could understand, for they also had come to look upon the men of the camp as friends, and the many bits of food that were thrown to them cemented the friendship.

In smaller cages were many little beasts and birds that the men had caught in their spare time – mongooses, honey badgers, jackals, bush-babies, wart-hogs, pelicans, storks, and secretary-birds.

Altogether it was a good collection. It had meant hard and sometimes dangerous work, but it was worth it.

The boys sat down to dinner with the contented feeling that they and their African friends had really done a job. They were all the more pleased because their father had been able to hobble out of his tent and join them at the table.

As they waited to be served, Hal noticed Joro half

hidden behind the tents talking with a black stranger.
They seemed to be arguing violently. The stranger drew
his knife and made such threatening gestures that Hal
almost rose from his seat to go to Joro's assistance. Then
he decided to wait and see what happened.

His father and Roger had their backs turned towards
this little drama. Hal alone could witness what was going
on.

The stranger seemed to win the argument. Joro at last
threw out his hands in a gesture that appeared to mean,
'Very well. I will do as you say.'

Then he went to the supply wagon and disappeared inside. In a few moments he was out again and wandered
over to the open fire, on which a pot of gazelle meat was
simmering – the stew that would very soon be brought to
the table. The cook was busy preparing other food. Joro
stood with his back to the pot and his hands behind him.

Could it be that he was dropping something into the
pot?

Presently he wandered away, his head down, his shoulders slumped. Whatever he had done, if he had done anything, he was not happy about it.

The cook had brought fruit to the table. Roger and his
father were eagerly devouring bananas and mangoes. Hal
did not eat.

'What's the matter?' Roger asked his brother. 'No
appetite?'

'Something funny is going on,' Hal said. 'Don't look
round.'

The cook ladled the gazelle stew out of the pot. He
brought the steaming dishes to the table and set them before the three hungry Hunts. Roger was about to dig in
when Hal said sharply:

'Wait!' Then he turned to his father. 'Dad, do you see anything wrong with this stew?'

'Why should there be?'

'It may be all right. But I thought I saw Joro put something into it.'

'It certainly smells good,' John Hunt said. He dipped up a spoonful and examined it carefully. 'No sign of any poison.'

'Hal is just imagining things,' Roger put in. 'Let's eat.'

'Hold it,' his father warned. 'What are these tiny bristles? They look like bits of stiff hair – chopped up.' He studied them for a moment. Then he said unhappily, 'I would never have believed Joro would do this.'

'Do what?' demanded Roger, impatient to get on with his meal.

'I'll explain later. Just now, I want to test Joro. I'm sure he's a leopard-man, but I still can't believe he would let us die. Act as if nothing was wrong. Pretend to eat – but don't.'

He stirred the fragrant stew, then took up a generous spoonful and raised it slowly to his lips.

'*Bwana!*' It was a sharp cry, and it came from Joro. He strode over to the table.

'What is it, Joro?'

'Two more hippos! They are on shore – not far away.'

'Don't bother me now,' John Hunt replied. 'After dinner we'll take a look at them.'

'But they will go into the river. Then it will be very hard to get them.'

'We can do better after we've had some food,' Hunt insisted. 'This smells mighty good.' He again made as if about to take some of the stew. Joro stopped him.

'No, no. It is *not* good. The cook made a mistake. He used bad meat. It is spoiled. It will make you sick.'

'Nonsense!' said Hunt. 'This gazelle was fresh-killed this morning. It's perfectly good.'

Joro grew more excited. 'I beg you – don't eat it.' But the three ignored him and bent over their dishes. Hysterically, Joro seized Roger's dish and emptied the contents on the ground. Then he did the same with the other two dishes. The cook came hurrying over to see what was wrong. Joro broke down, shaking and sobbing.

'I did it,' he confessed. 'The cook is not to blame. I did it. I put death in it.' He was trembling as if attacked by a violent fever.

John Hunt rose and put his hands on the black man's shaking shoulders.

'Pull yourself together, Joro. We understand. I know you are a leopard-man. I guessed it that night in the woods. I know how the Leopard Society works. They made you promise to kill us. Now it's all right – we didn't swallow any of the whiskers – so stop worrying.'

'Whiskers?' exclaimed Roger, staring as if he thought his father had gone off his head.

'Yes, whiskers. Joro, bring the leopard skin here.'

Joro hesitated. Then he went to the supply wagon and came back carrying the skin of the man-eating leopard that Hal had drowned on that first night of the safari.

John Hunt took the head in his hands and turned it so that the boys could look full into the beast's face.

'Do you see anything wrong?'

'It doesn't look quite natural,' Hal muttered, 'especially round the mouth.'

Roger guessed what made the difference. 'The hairs,' he

said, 'the stiff white hairs round its mouth – they're all gone.'

'Exactly. And you notice they weren't cut off. They were pulled out by the roots. Then they were chopped into small bits and and put into the stew.'

'But how could a few bits of hair hurt anybody? Are they poisonous?'

'Not at all. But they kill just the same. They don't dissolve in the stomach. They pierce the stomach wall and cause cysts. These become inflamed and lead to peritonitis. The Africans don't know the disease by name, but they do know that people die in terrible agony some time after swallowing leopards' whiskers.'

Hal saw Joro looking off into the bush. He followed his glance and spotted the black stranger. The man's face was full of anger and evil. Then he turned and ran.

Hal told his father what he had seen.

John Hunt said, 'He will probably report to the Leopard Society. He will tell them that Joro failed to carry out his pledge.'

'Then what will they do?'

'I don't know. One thing is certain. They'll do something, and whatever it is we're not going to like it. Keep your eyes skinned. If you see any sign of trouble, let me know.'

21 | Night attack

I T was an anxious afternoon.

The boys were busy preparing the cage trucks for the trip to the coast. But no matter how busy, they could not get rid of the uneasy feeling that they were in great danger. They watched warily for any black strangers lurking in the bushes. Roger hunched his shoulders.

'Any minute I expect to get a poisoned arrow in my back.'

Hour by hour they worked, and waited. The sun finally went down in a blaze of glory. There was a deep quiet over the plain, the woods, and the river. The birds peeped sleepily, a wart-hog sniffled, and the breeze made music in the long grass.

'Reckon nothing is going to happen after all,' hoped Roger.

'All the same,' Hal said, 'we'd better keep watch tonight. You bed down in the bushes at that side of the camp, I'll take the other.'

Roger went outside the ring of tents and made a nest for himself in the long grass. He tuned his ears to catch the slightest sound of approaching footsteps. This was rather exciting. He liked the idea of standing guard – especially if you could stand guard lying down.

An hour went by, and another hour, and he began to get drowsy. Then he slept, and dreamed.

He was standing guard on the battlements of a castle. Poisoned arrows were whizzing by him on all sides. It was not exactly a whizzing sound, more like a crackling – the crackling of fire. Then the castle, though it was built of solid stone, burst into flames. Roger woke.

There *was* a crackling. He stood up. There was a fire in the woods. The wind was carrying it towards the camp.

He heard another sound besides the crackling. It was the peculiar sawing voice of a leopard. It was joined by others. Now the sound came from all sides. The camp seemed to be completely surrounded by leopards.

Roger ran to his father's tent and found Hal already there, reporting on what he had seen and heard.

'They aren't leopards,' John Hunt said. 'They're the leopard-men. I'm afraid we have the whole Leopard Society moving in on us. And they're counting on the fire to help them. We may lose all our animals if that fire reaches them. Rouse the men. Have them drive the cage trucks over to the side of the camp away from the fire.'

'Do you think our crew will help us fight the leopard-men?' wondered Hal.

'Who knows? They're scared to death of leopard-men. Tell Joro to come here.'

A few moments after the boys had left, Joro entered.

'Joro,' John Hunt said, 'the time has come for you to decide whether you are with us or against us. If you help the leopard-men, you may save yourself and your wife and children. If you help us, they may kill both you and your family. I can't advise you what to do. But whatever you do, do it quickly.'

Joro did not answer. He turned and left the tent.

Motors were roaring. The cars were being moved to the safer side of camp. The entire woods were a sheet of flame and a steady wind brought it on towards the camp.

The leopard voices were now very close, and by the light of the fire leopard-clad figures could be seen coming out of the shrubbery. Roger was glad that at least they carried no bows and poisoned arrows. But he caught the flash of firelight on their long steel claws.

Of course they would not use arrows, for they considered that they had changed into real leopards. And a real leopard would use only his claws and teeth.

As they came rushing into camp, their smell came with them – the sour smell of leopard. For they had greased themselves from head to foot with leopard fat.

One of them came straight for Roger, claws outstretched. When he was within five feet, he leaped, as a leopard would leap upon an antelope.

Possibly he thought the boy would be an easy victim. But Roger, large and strong for his age and acquainted with some of the tricks of Japanese judo, flipped the flying body so that it came down with a whack on the stony ground. There the man who had thought himself a beast lay badly stunned. For a while at least he would give no more trouble.

Roger saw Hal, his face streaming with blood from scratches of steel claws, fighting three of the man-beasts. Roger plunged in to help him. He tripped one of the attackers so that he fell face down and Roger promptly sat on him. He could hardly stand the strong leopard stink that rose from the man's slippery hide. He saw that Hal had discouraged one of his assailants with a punch in the solar plexus and the other had run off to find an easier victim.

What about the safari men? They were not doing too well. Some fought half-heartedly, the others stood to one

side, shaking with fear. To them, these creatures with the
voices of leopards *were* leopards, or evil spirits, or both.
But Joro – Joro was fighting tooth and nail. He, himself a
leopard-man, was not fighting with the leopard-men.

He stood squarely in front of John Hunt's tent and
barred anyone who tried to enter. Skilfully he avoided the
flashing claws and hurled back every opponent until he
had a wriggling pile of them on the ground before him.
And all the time Joro shouted to the other safari men,
urging them to fight with him.

The tent flaps behind him opened and John Hunt came
out. He was weak and unsteady and in no condition to
fight. Joro roughly forced him back into the tent.

Another would-be fighter appeared, Colonel Bigg with
his gun. He fired two rounds, but his aim was so poor that
he nearly got safari men instead of leopard-men. At the
first scratch of steel claws he howled with pain and
dashed back into his tent.

But Hal, Roger, Joro, and two or three faithful safari
men could not hope to stand up to twenty steel-clawed
devils.

Then help came from an unexpected quarter. Three
hundred screaming baboons fled before the fire straight
towards the camp. The humans who had helped them
before perhaps would help them now. Driven mad with
fear, they poured into the camp ground.

But there they found the creatures they hated and
abhorred more than any others on earth. Their nostrils
were assailed by the sickening stench of their most deadly
enemies, the leopards. The horrible spotted hides were all
about them.

Every leopard skin drew the attack of a dozen baboons,
twenty, thirty, as many as could get their teeth into it.

The leopard-men ran for their lives. But wherever they ran, there were more baboons.

One of the now badly frightened human leopards noticed the open door of an empty elephant cage on one of the big Bedfords. He leaped through the door and was promptly followed by the other leopard-men.

Hal saw Joro running towards the cage. Was he going to join his leopard companions after all? But Joro had no such idea. He seized the cage door and swung it shut. Its automatic lock snapped.

The safari men, seeing twenty leopard-men behind bars, suddenly became very brave. These men or beasts or spirits could not have such magical powers after all, if iron bars could hold them. They crowded round the cage, screaming taunts and flinging pebbles at the prisoners.

The fire died out at the edge of the bare, stony camp ground. Tongues of fire licked on around the camp, terrifying the caged animals so that they gave out a wild chorus of screeches, snorts, hoots, croaks, and roars.

Their tumult died away when they found that they were safe from the flames, which raced on before the wind and would keep going until they reached bare sand or a river.

Joro went into the master's tent. Hunt's electric torch revealed torn clothes, bloody skin, and a happy smile. Joro looked as if the weight of the world had been lifted from his shoulders.

John Hunt felt a tide of affection for this man who had suffered and dared so much and had come through at last with flying colours. Here was a real friend if ever there was one. Hunt had a lump in his throat and did not trust himself to speak. Silently he reached up and gripped the former leopard-man's blood-stained hand.

22 | Elephant

DAWN saw the cage trucks on their way to the coast. Hal went along to superintend loading on to the ship.

The imprisoned leopard-men would be handed over to the police at Kampala.

At the same town the safari would see the last of Colonel Bigg and his gun. Probably he would brag to the end of his days about how he had fought off twenty devils single-handed and captured a magnificent collection of wild beasts.

The men not needed on the trip to Mombasa stayed in camp with Roger and his father.

'We'll have a surprise for Hal when he comes back,' said Hunt. 'Ever hear of the Mountains of the Moon?'

'Who hasn't?' exclaimed Roger. 'Land of the giants. Where flowers are as high as trees and even the worms are three feet long!'

'And elephants grow as big as mastodons,' Hunt added.

Roger saw the sparkle in his father's eye. 'I'll bet that's what you're after. Elephants. How soon do we start?'

'As soon as your brother comes back.'

So both Roger and the reader must wait a bit until Hal returns. The adventures of the Hunts in pursuit of the biggest of all land animals is told in *Elephant Adventure*.

If you have enjoyed this exciting adventure here are some others you may like to read, also published by Knight Books:

POST A LITTLE HAPPINESS

Post·A·Book